SOLVE FOR X

Christina Binu

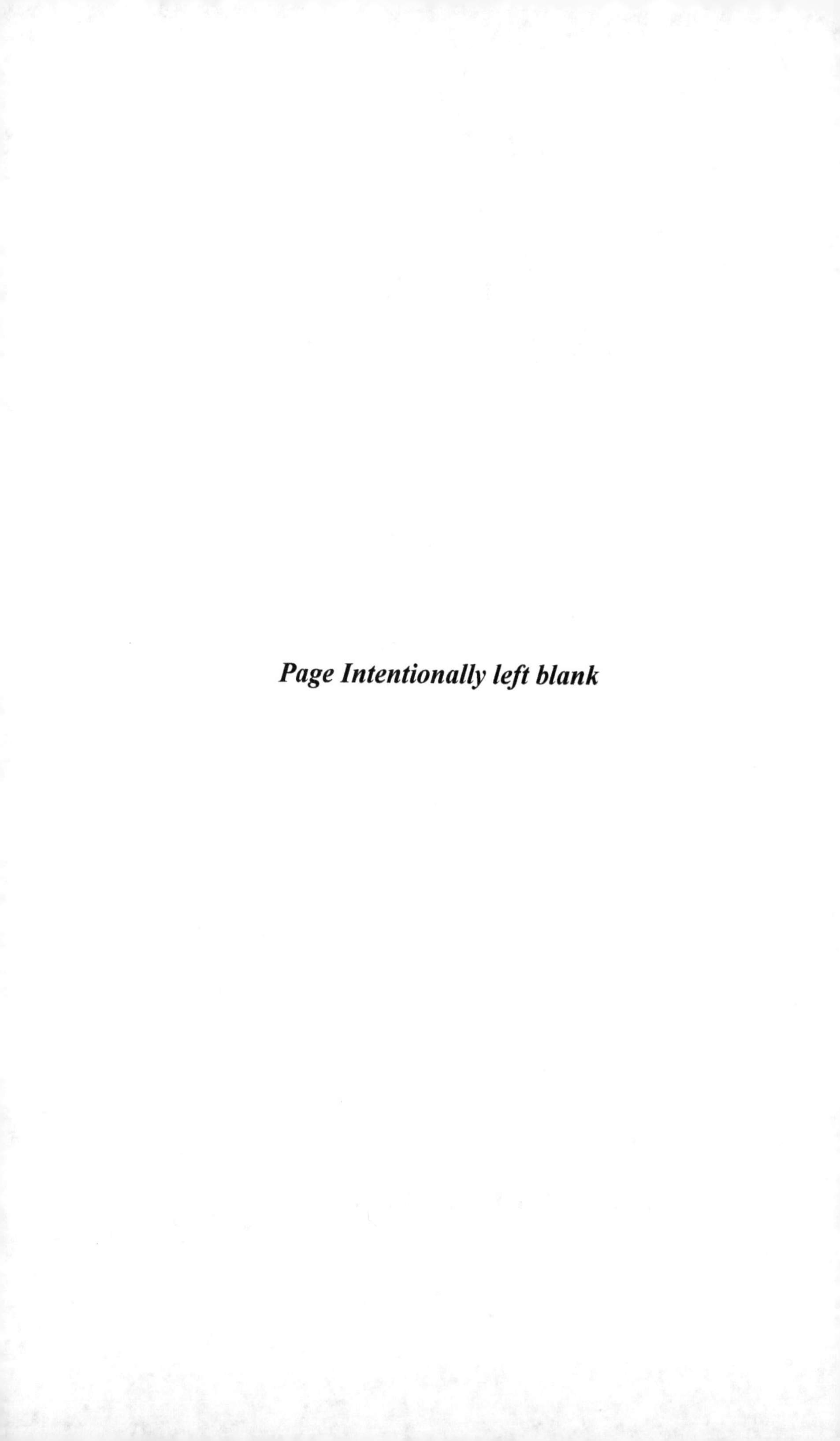*Page Intentionally left blank*

Copyrights

DEDICATION

To my ma and pa,

For your everlasting support.

AUTHOR'S NOTE

This story was not only a writing experience, but a whole new journey. It all started on the dawn of September 2023. I wish I remembered the date, but I don't. Every journey that I've ever started has given me so much to learn and experience. This one holds the title of my most unforgettable journey. No textbooks of mine, or the notes I had written staying up all night, had taught me how to create a whole new world with ink and paper.

Editing, Formatting, Cover designing, everything that I had to do on my own, doesn't count as a burden that I had to bear, but something new or exciting that I learned. As every journey has ups and downs, this one had too, accidentally deleting the only copy, rewriting a 'part' of the book for a whole year (crazy), but that's what, in a way, makes this journey unforgettable.

Table of Contents

CHAPTER 1 2

CHAPTER 2 6

CHAPTER 3 9

CHAPTER 4 16

CHAPTER 5 23

CHAPTER 6 26

CHAPTER 7 29

CHAPTER 8 34

CHAPTER 9 39

CHAPTER 10 41

CHAPTER 11 43

CHAPTER 12 53

CHAPTER 13 58

CHAPTER 14 62

CHAPTER 15 70

CHAPTER 16 80

CHAPTER 17 83

CHAPTER 18 86

CHAPTER 19 93

CHAPTER 20 97

CHAPTER 21 109

CHAPTER 22 115

CHAPTER 23 121

CHAPTER 24 125

CHAPTER 25 129

CHAPTER 26 135

CHAPTER 27 139

CHAPTER 28 142

CHAPTER 29 149

CHAPTER 30 155

CHAPTER 31 161

CHAPTER 32 168

PART ONE

CHAPTER 1

January 4th, 10:43 am

They say 'oh I want to be a child again,' or 'Oh, how happy I was when I was a child!'

But one winter consumed all my pleasure, and now the thought of going back to my childhood terrifies me now.

The end of fall was a few months ago, and winter knocked on the door again, an uninvited guest, but is never welcome. The courtyard, covered in perfect snow, as if it were a carpet laid, well, until mine and Amy's footprints ruined the scenery. Christmas shopping was never done, so was New Year's, or wouldn't have been done for at least a week after today, if Aunt hadn't noticed the expired boxes on the shelf. And, of course, Lena had to make her pay for not buying her whatever-shoes-it-is, *childish*. Elle had gone to help Aunt, especially to control Lena, as Aunt was spoiling her, and if she got out of control, she might bankrupt Aunt that very day.

The rays of light passed through the clouds that had covered the sky, and the sun shone through it, Amy was determined to make a snowman, but it was not as easy as you think, well, not for us. On our first try, the carrot, which they see as a nose, was falling off. I can't make out how a snowman's man can have such a long nose, or did they think he was Pinocchio? On the second try, we picked a comparatively smaller carrot, but the eyes made it look like it was the scarecrow in the fields. But hey, wouldn't a clay mould be much better than a 'snow' man? Why insist it must be snow?

Amy was not at all convinced she couldn't make one; she had made a bet with Lena, and I couldn't get her to give up on it, until I mentioned the project, the project we are supposed to submit tomorrow. We ran up the stairs, rushing to find the laptop, the textbook, searching on the internet for references, the laptop taking 2 minutes to turn on, never felt this long, ever. But at least it was not as hard as I thought it would be, as I had an expert right here, Amy. Don't know how, but she is excellent on computers and laptops, just, as it is.

She can search up things that would take a normal person hours to find, and somehow manages to find all the right things at the right time. And this time too, she was saying this too fast, faster than I could type. And at the right time, the battery was low. What was it? Murphy's law, isn't it? I wanted to break that laptop in half. But as a reminder, this laptop is not ours. Our teacher let us borrow hers. We could've asked our Aunt, but she's been busy these days, really busy. We didn't want to bother her.

A couple of knocks on the door, Aunt and others were back, right on time, now I don't have to do it all alone. I opened the door, and Elle's hands were occupied with a bunch of bags and groceries. I lent her a hand. Looked like Lena got what she wanted, too; there was a bag in her hand that she kept with herself, like we would have stolen it from her.

"There was a huge line in front of the counter, and it took forever!" Elle said, sitting on the couch, exhaustedly. She's been carrying this whole bag all the time, and she was tired. Lena carefully placed her bag in her room and came back.

"Can we make something? I'm starving," she said, and oh, I knew what was gonna happen...

"Em!" Aunt called me, as expected, "Help her make some snacks, I have some work to do, dinner will be ready soon after I finish it."

There have been situations like this, and all of them ended in a fight, if there really was anything that I and Lena could agree on together! I couldn't just dodge the fight, so I agreed.

Elle agreed to do the project when we were making snacks. But all I could remember was me and Lena getting into an argument over whether to make pancakes or popcorns, the next thing I knew was that my face was fully covered with flour, and I was holding a pan to hit Lena.

"What have you done? You have ruined a whole packet of flour!" Aunt was so done with us. "Well, it was because she threw popcorn at me!" Lena said with an innocent face. Yeah, like she isn't the one who started it.

But it all was fine, really, it was more than fine, more than I could ask for, a dodging from my nightmare, which had always been spending my youth in an orphanage, maybe there, I wouldn't even have the opportunity to fight or quarrel like this. This house was warm, not like winter, which always feels *cold*.

I am Emma, Emma Elizabeth Austin. Lena, Elisa, and Amy are my best friends, but that description feels distant. For my whole life, I've been with them; I can say that I grew up with them, precisely because we were family friends. Our families were neighbors, and our fathers were colleagues, or that's what my mom said. Our parents resigned very early, before we were born.

One January night, 10th January 2012, to be precise. One night was all it took. Our parents got into a car accident. This may be the only thing that I remember about that day, not that I remember; this is what others told me. Temporary memory loss, because of trauma, which was in my medical report. When police went to the accident site, a car that was burned to ashes wasn't the only thing they found; they found me, further from the accident site. I may have seen them dying, I may have seen the accident. But I don't remember. But how bad, oh God, I wish I remember.

Police didn't find the vehicle that hit them; they weren't able to. I remember glimpses of the police station, voices asking me what I had seen, or why I was there. Trust me, I wanted to know much more than they did.

CHAPTER 2

January 4th, 9:53 pm

Our parents died, leaving us to Aunt Ethal, Lena's Aunt. A nineteen-year-old girl had to look after four children, which might sound like.... what? Tiring? I don't know, but she did it anyway. She didn't have to; she could have left us in an orphanage nearby, or even left us in the streets, but all she did was to work, work tirelessly to look after us, and to maintain her studies at the same time. I often wonder how she did that. I have asked as well, but she never answered.

She always said it was the moon, though I don't really know what that means. A pale dead object, which have many cracks on its surface and is almost impossible to reach by an ordinary person, has been admired the most by philosophers, has been a listener to a broken, has been a symbol to love and beauty, has been a light to the lost, has been a subject of what birds sing of, has been a want of a silly child.

I climbed up the stairs, went to the balcony, and sat there until my mind was at ease. There was a cool breeze that was only found in winter. Christmas was over. But it didn't excite me even a bit. Christmas and New Year celebrations were one of the things we demolished after the accident. Just a week after the New Year celebration, we would have to celebrate our parents' death anniversary, so we didn't.

Every time I glance at other houses before Christmas, they have stars hung on top, a Christmas tree that has lights that could even light the whole world, a crib, that was the most inevitable for Christmas.

"It's time you went to bed," a voice startled me. It was Aunt. "But as you seem to be more thoughtful today, what happened? Do you need any help with the project?" she asked me, putting her hand on my shoulder. "You know about the project?" I asked, and everyone else agreed to keep that as a secret since we didn't want her to worry more by helping us; she has a lot of things to do than this.

"Your teacher told me, she called me this morning to ensure that you guys were preparing enough," She said, and that explained enough. "Em, I have been here with you girls for quite a lot time, right? I can know what you are thinking just from your face, you often come up here when you are desperate about something. I won't insist you tell me what or why, but you should know you're not the only one, you're not alone."

"Nothing, just thought about my mom and dad, and wanted to sit alone for a while, like people say, when someone dies they become a star, of course they would not, but I was just pushing my luck, who knows, what if they are actually listening," I said, and then left the balcony.

I walked towards my room. The same old cold breeze was blowing through my window. I opened the drawer to take a look at my family picture, the last gift my father had given me, which was their last photograph; they never had a chance to take another one.

I held that picture in my hands as a familiar creature entered the room, a butterfly, which had been here not once but also on the last December. It was crazy enough that a butterfly could survive in winter.

I tried to catch the butterfly, but it was some kind that I've never really seen before. I reached out my hands to catch it, but no, there suddenly came a screaming, not from outside, from my head, like it weighed a hundred pounds or something, a sudden dizziness. I wanted to call for help, but I couldn't. I fell into bed.

All I could do was to do nothing and stare at the ceiling.

CHAPTER 3

January 5th, 7:38 am

I opened my eyes again, and snowflakes stuck to my window; it was closed. There was no butterfly, no picture in my hands, nothing. I got up from my bed and walked towards the drawer. The picture was still there, with a sticky note beside it.

Told you not to leave your window open! It's snowing hard, and you could catch a cold. I've placed the breakfast on the table and packed your lunches. Have to leave early, Love you

Aunt.

I could imagine her face when she writes that, it's not the first time I left the window open. A smile came to my face as I read the sticky note again and again.

Lena rushed into my room. "And we've talked about entering the room without knocking, Lena!" I said, as I picked up the note that I dropped when she suddenly entered.

"Em, really? Check your phone, you dumb! We overslept!" Saying this, she rushed to her room, running to find her shoes, the uniform... And that was only when I checked my phone. 7:42?! Oh my- Our bus arrives at 8! Now I know why she freaked out like that, and now I am too.

Maybe it's because of the snowy night, we didn't even wake up to our alarms. Oh, not we, them, I didn't even get to put an alarm in the first place. We skipped breakfast, which has now become a not-so-healthy habit of ours.

But still, we missed the bus, we arrived ten minutes late, and now we have to wait for another twenty minutes to get another bus.

We usually walk to school, but not on snowy days like this. But waiting was still better than walking in this situation, as it takes forty minutes to reach school on foot.

***

When we arrived at the school gate, it was almost closing. Even though we were able to make it before the gate, we were sent to the principal's office for being late.

We slowly walked to the principal's office. As we passed through our own class, our classmates were staring at us. The boy, Sam, who we often call 'loudspeaker' for being too loud, announced, "Hey, the nerd siblings ain't absent!!"

As we walked into the principal's office, our principal, Miss Wanda, was on a call with someone. "Sir, this

is such a shock to us, but we'll highly cooperate with the–"
That is when she saw us standing in front of the door. We
may or may not have heard what she was saying.

She hung up the phone as soon as she saw us. "Why
are you girls standing there? Don't you know how to ask
permission?" she questioned with a frown. We simply said
we were late and asked her if we could go to class. As she
was disturbed by something else, all she replied was
"Whatever".

By the time we entered the class, it was the second
hour. "Hey bookworms!" Sam exclaimed. "Good morning,
loudspeaker," Lena replied with a grin on her face, as she
knew he really *hated* being called the loudspeaker.

"Looks like someone got detention," Millie, who
somehow doesn't really like us, muttered to her friend with
a not-so-beautiful giggle. "Well, looks like someone is happy
for our great achievement as getting a chance to meet Miss
Wanda early morning, and for that 'someone's' information,
we didn't get detention." Right when she was about to say
something, an English miss entered the class.

***

There was a break every two hours. During that
break, Crimson, yes, just like the color, which is the
'newspaper' of the school, came to us. She is a part of the
radio club, the speaker of our school radio program, and is a
good friend of ours.

"Hey! Did you hear the news?!" she exclaimed in
great surprise. "Of course, crimson, literally every single

rumor will only reach your ears first, how are we going to know?" I told her with a laugh.

"Oh come on! The whole school knows it by now, you know, the girl from the other class, Nora, apparently, she is not coming to school lately, and there are rumors that she is missing!" she informed us.

"Oh come on, Crimson, don't always follow the rumors," Amy, who was taking the notes, sneaked through the conversation.

"Don't always think that the rumors tell the story; they sometimes do. I'll tell you guys a secret, on the last day we saw Nora, her mother had called many students in our class to know if she was with them!" She whispered in a low voice. Before we could say anything, the bell rang. Everyone rushed into the class.

***

We entered the bus, which was almost empty. But it's lucky for us, we can sit anywhere. The rumors triggered some intuition of mine, but what possibly could've gone wrong? Chloe can get sick, Nora can too, can't they?

The cool breeze brushed my hair, as well as my thoughts. The small walk from the bus stop to home was quicker than usual. That walk was the most peaceful path for me. The tree in our courtyard was covered in snow, as were the other trees

***

We reached home by 5. I went straight to take a shower. The water was cold, colder than ever. As the cold water drenched me, slipping through my cheeks, my heart went back to the day when Nora came to school for the last time. That day, her mom had called me too, which I didn't take seriously until today. What I couldn't really make sure of yet was about the conversation Miss Wanda had on her phone. I recalled what she said lastly, "We will highly cooperate with the"

"Investigation," I told myself, it was a wild guess. I tried to connect the dots. Chloe and Nora are not coming to school for days,-missing, as per the rumors. "Maybe they are really–"

It took me a moment to find myself in a maze, "missing?" That was a question. I felt like I was drowning – in a bathtub? I let my face sink with my eyes closed. I woke up from some kind of a dream, with a scream, not mine.

It came from outside, so I went out to see what was happening. Amy looked disturbed. Lena was standing next to her, not tilting her gaze from our phone; there was Elle. No one said anything, and the room went silent.

I grabbed the phone from Amy's hand, a news report. "STUDENTS MURDERED." That heading just rang through my head. "Two students from Courtney International school have been murdered," *my school? Our school.*

STUDENTS MURDERED!

Two students from Courtney High School, Nora Smith and Chloe Fernandez, have been murdered. Nora Smith was reported missing by her family on 14th December. Police found her body on Meraine seashore on 15th December. As the family members requested, the investigation was kept confidential until this morning. Last night, Chloe Fernandez, another student from Courtney International School, was found murdered. About 8:40 this morning, the information about both murders was leaked from an unknown social media account.

That was all I needed, my head, heavy. I went back to the time when we walked into the principal's office, the phone call. It must have been the police on the other side.

"Elle," I broke the silence. "Crimson was right," I said, recalling what Crimson told us about both of them.

"I feel like I'm going to cry, Elle." Amy wanted to burst out all the emotions that disturbed her, even though we don't know those girls too much. My heart ached as I saw the news.

The next second, we heard a notification. It's from our school group.

Dear students, we hope you have heard the news about our beloved students Chloe and Nora. May God give their families strength to overcome this tragedy. Our school has decided to conduct a condolence meeting tomorrow, to show our grief towards the loss of our two brilliant students.

Principal, Miss Wanda.

My mind still hung on the word.

Murdered.

CHAPTER 4

January 5th, 6:44 pm

Our home was unusually silent this evening, everyone still in their own thoughts, as well as me.

A sudden doorbell woke me up from my thoughts. I stood up from the couch and went to open the door. It was Aunt.

"Sorry, girls, I forgot my keys today," she said, putting down the things she bought.

"There's good news," she said excitedly, except for the fact that two of our schoolmates were murdered. "You know the project I'm working on these days? It just got approved, and I've got a presentation tomorrow!" she said. It was good news, but she could read our faces.

"I'm sorry, girls, I just tried to cheer you up. I know about your classmates. I got the message from your class

16

teacher this morning. I've bought some bouquets for tomorrow, poor girls!"

That didn't light up the mood, but we had to go on, eat dinner, do homework, and then go to sleep.

I finished dinner fast and climbed up the stairs to my room. The same cold breeze, and a presence of someone, someone that I lost. I held my necklace in my hands, as tightly as the sharp corners of the snowflake's edge put a tear on my finger. It was my mom who gave me the necklace with a snowflake locket.

I didn't dampen my hold onto the necklace until a drop of blood fell onto my pillow. "Was not leaving me in this daze alone so hard, ma?" I asked as if she was hearing me from above the stars. I tried not to blame her. Is blaming a gone woman worth it? "Blaming yourself for something that wasn't in your control is also not something that's worth it," a voice in my heart echoed as a reply.

***

January 6th, 6:30 am

The sun had a bright ray this morning, unlike the cloudy days, being a blanket to our lazy thoughts. I woke up like I didn't sleep last night. I looked at the time, it was 6:30 am.

Today was the condolence meeting; today, we were told to wear a black dress. We didn't have classes. I climbed down the stairs, hearing the footsteps of my own. This place was never silent like this before.

I was the last one to wake up, or I might be the only one who slept. That's what Amy's face looked like, pale with dark circles under her eyes. She was holding a mug of coffee. She never liked coffee, let alone drinking it as the first thing in the morning. I gave her a confused look.

"A coffee a day keeps the sleep away," She said, reading the 'when did you even like coffee' question from my face.

The fact that Lena was wearing a black suit felt very different from what I've known; she was always a jolly person, the most colorful. She would always find a way to make things positive, even when we are supposed to be stressing out.

The familiar tensed expression on her face, I've seen it before, the day she knew our parents died. Elle is in the middle of cutting an apple, or is she? Because all she was doing right now was holding a knife and a half-cut apple and staring at the blank wall. *Distracted.*

"Everyone," I started the conversation first, "I can see everyone is a bit distracted, did Aunt leave early like usual?" I asked as a way of making everyone active as usual. "I'm here, Em!" Aunt came from behind, startling me.

"You're always scared, Emma, aren't you?" she asked and laughed.

Lena took an apple from Elle's hand and started to peel it. But to be honest, I doubt her peeling the whole apple because she was peeling too hard. She doesn't know how to peel an apple. Elle gave her 'Elle' look, the perfect elder sister look. She gazed at her like she was going to tear her in half.

I gave her an awkward smile and said, "Who needs to peel an apple when they have a big sister who can do it for you?". Lena repeated after me, "And who needs to clean this mess by themselves when they have the perfect, gorgeous sister?". Aunt was behind us, staring at all of this chaos. "Everything is fun until you are the one who is cleaning all this mess." Elle grabbed the apple in her hand.

"Has anyone told you that you're the best?" Lena was sugaring up Elle right now.

***

Unlike usual, Aunt dropped us. The compound was silent than ever before; there were black flags. We highly doubted whether there were people in there. Crimson approached us as soon as we walked past the entrance. The meeting was held in the auditorium. As we walked to the auditorium, I saw three chairs where the relatives of the deceased were seated. There were two men, who looked like they were in their early 50s, and a woman, whom I recognized.

It was Chloe's mother sitting farther from the corner; she was weeping, and looked like she hadn't eaten or slept well. The auditorium was silent and I could hear every single drop of tears falling down that mother's face. Unknowingly, I walked towards her. There was a man sitting next to her; he looked younger than Chloe's mother.

"Auntie," I sounded like my throat was on fire. She pointed her eyes towards me. I could tell that she was crying for a long time, hours, maybe.

"Were you close to my daughter?" she asked me, her voice was breaking in every word. "Did my Chloe cause any problem to anyone?! Has she offended anyone? Why! How could anyone do this!" She started screaming out loud, grabbing the collar of my black full sleeve shirt. I felt awkward; everyone was staring at me. The man, whom I assume is her husband, slowly grabbed Chloe's mother's hands, and he put his hand on her shoulder. I noticed the luxury watch on his hand, a golden chain on his neck, and a gold ring, 'rings', plural. There were 3 on his left hand and one on his right.

"Miss, you may calm down, Karma will always have its way to find the culprit," Miss Alice said to that lady. Suddenly, a hand grabbed mine and pulled me to the corner where our classmates were sitting, and that was Amy. I sat next to Crimson. She was whispering something.

"Crimson, where are Nora's parents?" I asked her, I couldn't see her mother, I had never seen her once, or did I recognize anyone who was related to Nora, they had never appeared at any PTA meeting. She pointed to the man in a black, neat shirt, with a leather jacket and a perfect tie as an answer. "That's her father," she made her voice less audible. "Her mother divorced her father like 4 years ago. I have heard that since then, she has never checked on Nora, but I can't believe she refused to come to her own daughter's funeral! Doesn't she even want to take a last glance at her daughter?" she exclaimed. "She doesn't even deserve a daughter!"

I felt pity for Nora and the man sitting there; he looked the most helpless. He has lost everything, his wife, his only daughter, everything. "*Pathetic*," I said, thinking about that man; at the end of the day, he is a father.

"And I assume that man consoling Chloe's mother is her husband, Chloe's dad?" I pointed to the man sitting next to Chloe's mother, and he hugged her, crying with her. "Is their family rich?" I asked, keeping in mind that he wore 4 gold rings on his daughter's mourning ceremony. "Rich? They're like *rich, rich*, they may own the whole city!" She made her voice a bit higher.

Suddenly, Miss Wanda took the mic and started speaking. "Our two stars of this school, Nora and Chloe, have now left us for another world. By conducting this ceremony here, there are a few people who would like to speak about Nora and Chloe and share–" As she was speaking, I could see Crimson was murmuring to Lena about something. About the same thing she was talking to before.

"What are you talking about?" I asked, whispering in her ears. "About Sarah and Claire, they were like best friends since childhood, but something happened 4 years ago, teachers changed their divisions, and they have never talked to each other since then. Their whole families are rich; one literally owns a company, and Claire's family is engaged in real estate. I can't believe they didn't show up."

Four years ago... The year Nora's mother divorced her father. There was definitely something fishy about Sarah and Claire.

I went out secretly from the hall to the girls' washroom, took out my phone from my pocket. Phone wasn't allowed on the campus, and I knew it. The first thing I searched was 'Nora Smith'; nothing came up. Then I tried 'Chloe Fernandez', still nothing.

Suddenly, a girl's voice jumped in the air, "What?" She paused, "Are you trying to do without us… you 'know it all'

"Nothing to be calm, it's all serious!" I handed my phone to Amy. "Go on, smart head, I need something about Nora and Chloe," I told her. "Is this about that Sarah and Claire?" Lena knew exactly where I was going. "Nothing" that got my attention, "There is nothing about Nora and Chloe in the internet.

"Look, Em, there is nothing serious like you said," Elle said, washing her hands, which were covered in… paint? I tried not to keep my attention on it and said, "Exactly! That nothing IS something, two high school girls, murdered weeks ago, and there's *nothing*! Where is the news we saw about them yesterday?" I asked Amy.

"Removed," I said along with Amy. Just like I guessed.

CHAPTER 5

January 6th, 12:02 pm

We reached home by noon, the ceremony was over. Walking through the same path, which was utterly a distraction for me once, is now filled with my thoughts and intuitions. I'm not a detective, not a police officer either, not a lawyer, nor the judge, not close to Nora that much, maybe even less than I am close to Chloe.

But my mind was still circling around everything that's happening these days, the rumors, or maybe even the truths, Crimson has told me. Unlike usual, or never once, our front door was open. Did Aunt forget to lock the door? Lena went in to see what was happening in there. She came out after a couple of minutes.

"Nothing." That was what she said. "Nothing is stolen, nothing is broken, nothing!" She continued. "And I clearly remember Aunt locking the door," Elle promised.

"Should we call someone?" Amy was still concerned. "I don't think so, since there is nothing wrong inside, I don't think we should," Lena told us.

I entered our house, much consciously than usual. To my surprise, everything was in its place just like we'd left it in the morning. The windows were closed, and the curtains were placed in the same position; the chairs around the dining table were too. When I woke up this morning and came here, the chair I pulled out was positioned towards the east, and it was the same when we left. Another, on which Lena had taken as a support to take the snacks from the shelf, much taller than her, was in the same position, too. I recalled every minute detail of this room when we left, everything looked like it hadn't moved. There was no evidence of a person entering the room.

I climbed up the stairs, unaware of what I was looking for; in fact, Elle wasn't the only one who remembered Aunt locking the house. I saw that too. I went to my room, and everything was the same as before; the books on the couch were in the same position as before. Everything looked right until… I entered my room.

Nothing seemed to have been touched, from a quick look, nothing, except for the fact that the drawer I had left closed was opened by someone. I frantically opened the drawer. As I had expected, the only valuable thing in the drawer was a family picture, mine.

How could someone break into a house just for a picture, and it is obvious that the thief knew exactly where it was placed? There were no signs of an inspection.

"You're wrong, Lena!" I said, loud enough for the whole city to hear, "They took my family picture!"

"Your family picture? Why would someone need your family picture?" Amy didn't believe me at first. "You sure you didn't misplace it?" Elle continued.

"How can I have misplaced a thing when I haven't touched it?" I asked them. I was damn sure I didn't 'misplace' the picture. It was the most valuable thing for me. The only thing my dad has left me with. I could practically *see* how he handed me the picture. Right before leaving the house, he picked me up and handed me the photo, "To my beautiful daughter as an early birthday gift, who knows, maybe I wouldn't make it till October!" It was a joke, a painful one, it's like me, my father, and I am good at having intuitions, and I believe the last one he knew was his death.

I went through every chance of where my picture could be, but no, it is not here.

CHAPTER 6

January 6th, 6:54 pm

Aunt came home early today, too. She was happier than usual. The second she came home, she threw her bag and hugged us in joy. "The project is approved!" She was technically dancing with happiness. "But I have to make sure of one thing: my company has arranged a business trip that I can't avoid. I'll be gone for 2 weeks, so promise me you won't get into any trouble, would you?" She told us. "But I don't think that would actually work because wherever Lena is, there is chaos," I replied, and Lena was so not happy about that statement. We ran around the house to see who would catch whom first. "Now, you two, stop turning the damn house upside down, would you?" She was so done with us. We didn't mention my family picture; we didn't want to change the happy mode.

Aunt went to her room to get fresh. "Are we not going to talk about the theft?" Amy whispered. "Never!

She's already worried about us getting in trouble while she's gone, don't even think about it; she may even cancel the trip!" Lena said out loud. I covered her mouth with actual tape.

***

We ran into our room and locked the door. Suddenly, I noticed a scratch of paint on Elisa's thumb; I remembered her getting her hand full of paint this morning. "Elle," I called her. "What's that on your thumb?" It seems like she only noticed it when I asked her. "Oh, I thought I had all the paint removed. I ran into a boy today who was carrying paint; thank God I didn't get any paint on my dress." She replied.

A boy with a paint bucket? As far as I know, our school wasn't under maintenance; there was no other reason a boy should carry a paint bucket while a condolence ceremony was going on. "Have you seen him anywhere?" I asked her. "No, never. Now you've asked, I wonder who he was too, although he was wearing a mask so that I couldn't see his face," she replied. I couldn't know why I was getting suspicious about everything that was happening nowadays.

Suddenly, something got my attention. Our house was locked. Elle was given the spare key. There was no evidence of someone breaking the doorknob. Elle bumped into a never-seen-in-entire-life guy. Things started to make sense. "Elle," I called her again, this time more frantically. "Don't you have the spare key with you?" That was the only time she thought about the spare key. "Yes, I did." She went to get her black coat from her closet. She checked the pockets again and again. "It isn't there, is it?" I knew exactly how a person got into our house without leaving any traces of being forcefully opened. But who? Why? How did he know where exactly my family picture was placed? For a second, I was having a headache, feeling burnt out.

I went to my room. Staring at the empty drawer, I sighed. My sigh echoed in the silence. The wind crawled into my room. I held my necklace again. "Pa, I lost our photo." I walked towards the window. The curtain danced as the breeze went out, brushing my hair.

CHAPTER 7

January 7th, 2022, 6:27 am

Aunt left early morning; she had her flight at 5 in the morning. I remember waking up when she was leaving, at 3:30 am. I didn't go back to sleep; I couldn't. I could hear Elle cooking. Since Aunt wasn't here, she was the one who was preparing food. I went to help her.

We got ready and went to school earlier than before. It was a Saturday, but we had special classes since final exams were coming. This time, we locked the door from inside and came outside through the back door and locked it; it had a different key. The same path from home to the bus stop felt longer. The sky was cloudy. The trees on either side of the roads were washed in snow.

We entered the class, and Chloe's seat was left empty. "Her mom came and took her things yesterday," Crimson told us. There was an odd silence. I could hear the steps of the wind climbing through the windows. We went to our seats.

I have never felt like this before, and I don't know what I am feeling. Pity? Curious? The class was only till noon. I had lost my way in thought, and I never noticed the class had ended until someone touched my shoulder, Amy. I came back to reality, like I just woke up from a nap.

"Hey, I noticed you were really distracted in class. I know a lot's going on in your mind, but we have to go on, right? We've got final exams coming, nothing's gonna change." She was right, nothing's going to change. Even though two students of our school were *murdered*, nothing's going to change, huh?

"She's right, Emma," I heard another voice, Sam's. It was the first time I heard him call my real name. "And oh, right, you've got some letters, I've put them in your locker," He said. There is a school post office in our school, quite strange, but it's a good thing. The letters of admission, scholarships, or anything that is to be given to a student will be put in their locker, and Sam is in charge of that. This thing is quite useful because if you want to curse someone anonymously, this is your chance, though that is prohibited after a student wrote something to a teacher here.

I went to my locker while others waited for me in the corridor. There were a couple of letters, one from the scholarship that I applied to, well, not that much in it, I just got declined. Then, there was one from an anonymous messenger.

'Find me if you can, Emma Elizabeth Austin!'

That was the letter, just one sentence, but why would someone write to me? Why do I feel like the handwriting… I know this handwriting. But no matter how hard I tried, I couldn't remember whose.

There was another letter in the locker, but I didn't open it. I crumbled all the letters and put them in my bag.

I rushed towards Amy, Elle, and Lena and dragged them to the girls' toilet. "I might sound crazy, but we need to find out what is going on behind those two murders!" I said. I didn't tell them about the letter.

"When you said you might sound crazy, I didn't think you would spit absolute rubbish," Elle immediately responded.

"I am for real! If I don't figure it out myself, I might lose my mind! Every second, my mind is circling around the moment I saw Chloe's mom, and the things Crimson told us are repeating over and over in my mind. Who would kill two random kids out of nowhere? Moreover, do you think the theft yesterday was just a 'theft'? Who would know where I have placed my stuff? Who knows, maybe I, or even us, can be his next target!

I was shouting, and Lena covered my mouth. The next second, we heard something fall on the floor. It was crimson. "Oh my, can I join you too?" That was the most realistic response since it was from Crimson.

"Em! Look what you have done! We are not detectives, are we?" Elle was so done with me. But no one can convince my reasonable sister to do unreasonable things better than I. As for the case of crimson, even God can't convince her to give up something, so I didn't bother telling her to forget what I had said. As long as I am not a mermaid who can erase memories, that is all I can do.

***

We reached home. Amy was looking for the case details on the internet.

"As expected, nothing on the internet, just the things we know, such as Nora being murdered on 14th December and found at Meraine seashore, and Chloe found on 4th January, we yet don't know where they found her, the rest is just groundless rumors," She said with a disappointed face.

Some things rushed to my mind as I heard the dates. It was on 14th December that the butterfly came into my room for the first time, and it was also the first time I got headaches after a long time. Then it was 4th January, just some days ago, when it came to my room the second time. Was all this merely a coincidence?

"It is good to know something; it is still better than nothing. We need to make our way through the things we have now. What about going to the seashore? Moreover, it is not far away from our home, is it?" I told them not to reveal the butterfly. Elle already thinks that I am crazy with the investigation idea; if I tell her about this, she might confirm it.

"That seashore is sealed; no one is allowed to get in there," Elisa reminded us. "Does anyone have to teach us how to sneak in? Lena said as she put on her jacket. "But it's already 8 pm," Amy said. She looked nervous. "Looks like a perfect time to sneak in on me," Lena walked towards the

32

door. I followed her, grabbing my jacket. Elle and Amy followed us.

A particularly cold night. The wind was blowing harshly.

We managed to get to the seashore, but the wind was making us blind. In the darkness, I saw a shadow. I grabbed everyone else and hid behind something, a rock maybe. The shadow was getting closer and closer. I held my breath. The wind slowly revealed the man. A tall figure, I couldn't see his face. He was holding something, a wine bottle? Who would drink at a sealed seashore in the middle of the night? The moonlight shone through the darkness that had covered his face. Sharp eyes. "What are you doing here, kids?" the rough sound of a beast.

CHAPTER 8

January 7th, 9:12 pm

"Plan b," I whispered under the silence. "What the hell is your plan B?" Elle is so going to kill me. I counted to three. "RUN!!" I shouted. We ran as fast as we could. Amy was screaming loudly. My long, wavy hair, which was let free in the wind, blocked my eyesight. I tied it with a hair tie I was wearing in my hand. I looked behind. We were not that far from the seashore. The tall shadow stood there watching us run. It took me a moment to regain my mobility. Elle, who had run faster, came back and grabbed my hand and started running again.

The houses on either side of the road light up at the sound of Amy's scream.

We reached home, and I opened the door as fast as I could. Thank Goodness I didn't break the doorknob. We closed the door and double-locked it. I could hear my heartbeat every second. Elle went to the kitchen and drank a bottle of water.

"Em, your brilliant idea almost killed us!" Amy shouted. "The plan of sneaking in was not mine!" I said, looking at Lena. "Is this what I get for backing up your plan? Everything must have gone well if that man wasn't there!" She said.

"Can you guys shut up for a second?" Elle burst out of anger. "What if that man is the one who killed Nora and Chloe? What would have happened to us if he had caught us?" She was fed up with all this.

"He won't," I said, "At least he wouldn't, and when I looked back, I saw him watching us run. If he had any plan to kill us that moment, he could have done that; we wouldn't have reached home by now, but instead, he just watched."

Everyone paused. I stepped towards the stairs, marching towards my room. A disappointing night, I should've been delighted that I didn't get kidnapped by a mysterious figure. I opened the windows, inviting my frequent guest. Wind greeted me by touching my emotionless face. I exchanged smiles with the moon. It was a crescent moon, brighter than ever.

"Ma, do you think, do you think I am acting recklessly? Maybe I got too emotional about our photo." My eyes were tearing up. "But I won't let it go easily, I am damn sure the theft of our photo has something to do with you and dad, right? Maybe no one else would believe your accident wasn't really an 'accident'. What if the murderer has some connections with your case? Or else how would anyone know about our family picture? Moreover, who would it benefit by getting our family picture? And the letter, I'm sure it isn't any pranks or something, Pa, I wish you were here. Every time I was stuck in a puzzle or a riddle, you would pop up and easily solve it.

I will go to check on that seashore again. I don't care if they can accompany me; in other words, I shouldn't drag them into trouble.

***

January 8th, 2022, 5:33 am

I sneaked out through the back door, taking my phone with me. It was cold in the morning. I woke up as early as I could so that I wouldn't notify them. As it was a Sunday, they might sleep longer. The moon was still there. Looks like it really heard me last night. As I walked towards the shore, I saw the same tall figure again. This time, I hid behind a rock. Did he stay here the whole night?

"Why is he here again?" A voice jumped out from the bush behind me. "Shh! She might hear us!" another voice, Elle's. I removed the bush. Lena was smiling awkwardly. "Don't you think you were a little loud?" I asked her. Suddenly, they looked behind me with scared faces. "What? Is there a ghost behind me?" I asked them.

"Indeed, a ghost," the rough, low-pitched sound behind me scared me to death. A hand pushed me behind, grabbing the collar of my blue jacket. "Do I look like a ghost?" He asked. He wasn't, indeed.

"Well...." I was at the awkward and scariest moment of all time, "You… you don't look like a ghost at all, right?" I turned to others who were trying to run. "There is no use in running away, and how can you be sure that I won't eat your friend alive?" I don't know if he was for real. He let go of his hold on my collar, and I rushed towards others.

"Why did you turn to us?" Lena whispered under her breath. "If I am going down, I'll drag you down too; moreover, who told you to follow me?" I told her.

"Hey! You kids, why are you here, at a sealed seashore? Do you know the consequences?" he started to talk. "Before teaching us about the consequences, why won't you look at yourself? You are the same, standing at a sealed seashore," I said back.

"Then why won't you tell me why you are here? You sure don't look like the ones who would come to a sealed seashore just because of a dare. Let's look for a compromise, I won't report you," He said, looking at me. "Why would we?" Elle interrupted him. "How can we make sure you are not the one who killed those students?"

He gave her a sarcastic laugh and then took out his ID from his pocket. "Private detective?" Amazed, I stared at Elle. "I am Jack, the private detective assigned by Nora's family to investigate the case. They seem to be not unsatisfied with the police investigation. As for the accusation you have made, that I have sneaked into a sealed property, as the person who is investigating the case, I have the authority to visit the crime scene. Now I look into the situation, you are the only ones who have sneaked into a sealed property, and as for your accusation, if I took it as an offense, you would be screwed," He said.

Now I have the feeling that I have *actually* brought up a problem. "I have cleared myself, now I will give a chance to clear as well as you, too." his stubborn voice was loud enough to pierce my ears. "Okay," Lena stepped forward with a righteous look. "We…. We are from the same school as the victims, and we thought we could investigate the case ourselves as we wanted to find out who was behind it." She could at least act like being reasonable, but now that I am hearing my own idea, I feel like the most unreasonable person in the whole world.

"These kids nowadays," he whispered to himself, "If you really want to help your dead friends, the best you could do is to cooperate with the investigation of the police. But if you really go after this case, not only will it affect your studies, but also will get you in trouble like this, I will let you girls go this time. But if you go after it again, I am afraid I can't favor you all anymore."

He was right. I might get in trouble for this, but who knows if I won't, even if I don't look into it?

CHAPTER 9

January 8th, 11:42 am

I went to the public library, looking for that specific butterfly in every single book I could see that was about butterflies. It was strange enough that I had never seen it before. I searched through bookshelves and bookshelves, books after books about butterflies. About the poisonous ones, about the ones that can survive in winter, but there were none that looked like the one I saw.

I never believed in ghosts, but now I am nearly convinced that they were the souls of those students. Logically, there's no explanation other than that the butterfly is a rare variety that has never been found, and those dates were just coincidences. But coincidences don't happen that often, and I can't be as lucky as to be the first one to discover a freaking new species.

I leaned towards a wall of that library, sitting between the shelves. I had my Rubik's Cube with me. Took it out and started to solve it, but every time, just when I reached the last step, I would mess up. It happened a couple of times. This time, I stopped when I reached the last step and put down the Rubik's Cube.

A book fell from somewhere all of a sudden. A guy just popped up from nowhere and took my Rubik's Cube. "Solving a Rubik's cube in a library, interesting though. But why is it left unfinished?" He asked.

"I am afraid of messing it up, so I just left it like that," I said. "Why leave it unfinished when you have only one step ahead? You won't know until you try." Saying this, he left, giving me a book. There was a note on top: *I can see that you're looking for butterflies, even though I don't know what you are looking for, as you have not found it among the alive ones, maybe look for the dead ones, and you have pretty Hazel eyes, Will.* It was a book about extinct butterflies.

Even though there was no information about the butterfly that I was looking for, I solved the Rubik's Cube.

CHAPTER 10

January 8th, 7:49 pm

It was already evening when I came back, and I had to spend a couple of hours in front of a shop because they were selling Lena's favorite drinks at half price today. I entered the house, and the lights were off. I walked towards the switch and turned it on. "Ah! Jesus, why are you all sitting here with the lights off? Gave me a heart attack, might as well kill me too!"

"We didn't," Elle whispered.

"What?"

"We didn't turn off the lights, the lights, they've been turning on and off for hours now! Oh my – Em, can it be that the killer is now aiming at us?" Amy said nervously.

"What happened? Why would you say that? Look, we are not related to this whole mess; we just have to find that killer, and it's all over," I replied.

"Remember, Crimson told us about Sarah and Claire? We looked up about them, but things are not clear, four years ago, they were best friends, the four-member group of theirs, were well known, they were excellent in everything, but the year before we joined… something happened, that isn't even on the records, Amy hacked the school system, but there were none, that 'something' made everything change, they changed classes, and no one has seen them together since then" Lena said.

I silently sat there, hearing all those things. I felt something, like something was pushing me, a pain in my chest. "I have to go," I stood up from my chair. Unusually, my steps were unbalanced. "Em, you okay?" I heard a voice; it echoed through my head, and it was heavier than ever. I didn't bother to reply. I climbed up the stairs as fast as I could; my head was bouncing, dizzy, and I walked to my room. The window was open. I fell onto the bed.

CHAPTER 11

January 9th, 7:45 am

I woke up from a shock. It was a Monday. I stood up, still feeling dizzy, and I held Lena's hand. She was the one who woke me up. I looked confused. My eyes took a glance around my own room, like I was searching for something, someone.

"Em, did you hit your head or something? You walked out of the discussion without saying a word, now you look like you have lost your memory." She asked me.

"Don't we have class?" I asked with a sore throat. My head was aching. "Yes, we do, and you are late; you are the only one left to get ready! If we are late again, I don't think Miss Wanda is going to let us go like the last time." I rushed to the bathroom. "You guys can leave first," I said loudly before going to get ready.

I clearly had a cold, but I didn't care. It was already late when I left the house. I was running through the snow-covered path to the school.

I reached the gate, panting, and the gate was closed. We get fined for being late, and only after paying the fine will I be able to attend the classes. I knew I would be late, so I had already carried the fine with me. I again missed the first hour. I was tired after running so many miles. I felt like I was going to faint. I was coughing all the way to class. It was history hour. I slept throughout the class, not because it was boring.

The teacher noticed me. I was so deep into sleep that I didn't even hear Amy calling me. I suddenly woke up after she shook me. I looked at the teacher, who seemed like a devil to me at that time. "Are you feeling sleepy, Emma?" Oh no, this is bad, how to get out of trouble. "No, Miss, really, I am not. It is just I was-" she cut me off in the middle. "Did you catch a cold?" She checked my temperature. 104°F.

***

I was sent to the school clinic to get cold medicines. I walked into the school clinic. The school nurse was putting stickers on medicine bottles that had the names of the medicines on them. Seems like she didn't notice me coming in. "Shall I help?" I asked with a mild voice. She was surprised to suddenly hear my voice. "Oh, I didn't notice you coming in. What are you here for?" Her smile was contagious. "I need some cold medicines," I replied.

My voice had changed due to the cold. After checking my temperature again, she told me that I needed rest. She returned to naming the medicines. I insisted on helping her, so she agreed and gave me some medicine bottles.

While I was doing that, the bell rang; it was interval time. Soon after the bell rang, Amy rushed into the clinic, grabbed my hand, and started running. She paused for a moment, looked back at the nurse, and said, "I really need her now."

I was invisible to the situation. Why is she running like that? "Amy, had the time stopped? Or is the world crashing down?" I stooped and dragged her back. "If you don't come now, the world might crash now!" she yelled.

When she stopped, it was the corridor. She covered my mouth and pointed to two girls who were talking to each other, nervously. I could guess that it was Claire and Sarah. Elisa and Lena were also there. We walked towards them. Crimson was in the hallway, too.

When we approached them, I heard crimson whispering to Sam, "Hey, loudspeaker! Watch how the hallway is going to explode!" Just like she said, the hallway almost exploded. The "Talk" we had ended up in a fight. The corridor was crowded. Students gathered to see the fight.

After a few seconds, the teacher rushed into the crowd. "You girls! Do you think you are street fighters, huh? Lena, Elisa, Amy, Emma, four of you! To the principal's office, now!"

Did they forget those two's name or what? The teacher shouted like we four were the only ones there. It is not like they are invisible, right? I was so furious.

We walked towards the principal's office. She was talking to someone else… Jack? We sat on the bench outside the office. After a while, she got a call and went to another room. Only then did he notice us. It was like he couldn't control his laughter. "You girls got into trouble, didn't you? I gave some advice to you all yesterday, and look at you, you got into trouble the next day." I could read through his look at what he was going to say.

"Jack! Over here!" Lena called out. Elle pinched her, hinting not to do that; she wouldn't listen, so do I. My sore throat didn't let me say things loud enough, but I managed to say that we needed his number. But he couldn't hear it properly. I had to repeat it again and again until I lost my temper. "Not humble you, Idiot! Your *number*!" I shouted with all my might. Fantastic. Now I can't say a word. I completely lost my voice.

"What did you call me? I am your elder; you should at least not call me by my first name, but now you're calling me an idiot? Where are your manners ……." and so on, he continued his lecture while the time was ticking. If Miss Wanda hears any noise from here, we are doomed. Misery loves company, here she is! Couldn't she hold the call for a couple more minutes?

We became silent. She glanced at us and entered her office. She and Jack seemed to have a serious conversation. After a while, Jack came out of the office and walked away as if he had never known us. We were the next prey of Miss Wanda.

"You should know that we have a really great reputation. Fighting with your peers is not acceptable. What happened to you four? You have contributed much to the school, but for some weeks, you girls have been getting into trouble again and again. Considering your character before, I will cut off the detention by 50 pages. You should submit it tomorrow. Got it?!" She was so fed up with us, but we are not the only ones, are we? They didn't punish those two students.

We walked towards our class. We could hear whispers all the way there. The class became silent when we entered. Millie got up from her seat. "Looks like someone got suspended," she said out loud.

"Bookworms! But what did you do to get suspended? Will Miss Wanda suspend you for a class fight?" Sam joined. "First of all, we didn't get detention, and secondly, I heard someone told Miss Wanda that we were the ones who started the fight, for that person's attention." Lena glared at Millie. "I know you might be disappointed with our punishment, well, you have to try harder next time you frame someone."

"Lena! What do you mean by that? You can't just accuse me of something that I don't even know," She flared up the second Lena glared at her.

"I never said it was you, and honestly," Lena came closer to her and whispered, "Don't think you can put up this act forever". At that time, I was so fed up with her that I forgot what we were truly after. Jack was going to leave the school. We had to stop him and ask about the case.

I truly wanted to help those students who died in vain. And I am pretty much sure my past has something to do with this. Maybe I can remember what happened that night. And of course, there's a gut feeling that tells me that those letters aren't some pranks.

We followed him all the way to the ground. "Hey! We have wasted our interval time getting your number; at least you can give us some information. How can you know if we are troublemakers if you don't know us?" Lena asked him. Even though he was walking non-stop because he knew we were behind him, he stopped at that moment and came back.

"It's not because of you all being troublemakers, as a stranger, you should stay away from me, and secondly, I can't just get some students to be involved in a murder case, it is dangerous than you think. At that time, I stepped forward and tried my best to speak.

"Look, it's not like we have not witnessed even more dangerous things than this, I… I witnessed our parents turn into ashes, and for their sake, I have been keeping a family photo that I lost the other day. It was not a mere robbery, nor did I lose it carelessly; a never-ever-seen person stole our keys to open our house, but he didn't even touch any of the valuable things except for that photo, and he knew exactly where it was kept.

You might ask how these two cases are connected, but trust me, it is not a coincidence. They, our fathers, used to be colleagues; they were police officers, until they suddenly resigned together, even before we were born, I

Suddenly, he cut me off in the middle. "Wait, your father's name is…?" He asked as if something triggered. "Austin, Austin Alexander, do you…. Do you know him?" I asked him. He paused for a moment. "No wonder you looked familiar," he whispered under his breath.

We heard the bell ringing, so we had to go back to our classes. "Come meet me at the same seashore," He said, staring at me confusingly. "Weren't you the one who told us trespassing on a sealed property is illegal?" Lena spoke up. "Does it even matter now? You've already been there, even if you've been there twice or thrice, the punishment will be the same." Saying this, he walked out of the compound.

"What a tough nut to crack," Amy whispered all the way to the class.

***

I've got another letter, but this time, it is different.

Greetings, Emma Elizabeth Austin,

I can see that you are worn out trying to figure out who the murderer is, then let me tell you a secret… Look at the archive box, and then you might find something really interesting!

Hunter

The handwriting in the letter that I received first is different; someone else wrote it, and whoever it is, they know something. Someone who wants the murderer to be caught? The school archive box… where they dispose of letters after reading.

*****

I went to the archives without telling anyone. No one is allowed to take letters from archives except the person in charge, who is Sam, and then they burn the letters (Valuable letters, like about scholarships and others, should not be disposed of)

As I walked towards the Archive room, Sam was taking out the letters.

"Hey Sam!" I called him. "Miss Wanda is calling you, she said It's urgent," I lied, but I had to get my hands on the letters no matter what.

"Oh, I was just about to take these out," He said.

"That's fine, friends help each other, right? I can take these out for you; you'd better go see Miss Wanda."

"That's not like you, Emma, but yeah, sure, since you want to help, but make sure no one knows, or me and you, both of us gonna get detention," He said, passing the box to me.

"Of course I know the rules, not gonna tell a single soul." *Except for the fact that I am going to open every single one of these.*

I quickly went to the post office and then locked the door. I put down the box in one of the tables and then took one of the stacks placed in it. There were several other stacks, which I had to check one by one. Oh, this is *not* going to be an easy job.

There was a knock on the door. Did Sam come back? Did he know that I lied? No, it can't be, there isn't enough time for him to go to the office and come back within this short time. Or is it someone else? No, someone else can't see me here, or else I'm doomed.

"Emma! We know it's you, it's Elle." Oh, I almost had a heart attack. I opened the door.

"Would you mind explaining why you are in the post office with the box of archives, when both entering the office and handling the archives are prohibited for normal students?" Amy asked.

"And for whatever reason, it is, it's too dumb for you to lock yourself in the post office itself, what if someone sees you! Quick, let's go to the back." Lena grabbed me and we went to the backside of the building, also known as Block E. Every school has a prohibited area, and ours is Block E. Not many go there during the daytime, some go there as 'Dare' or something because of the rumors (That it is haunted or something).

"So now, would you tell me why?" Elle asked.

"Um, guys, sorry for not telling you, but I received some letters and–" I handed them the letters.

"The handwriting, in the first one… It's a bit"

"Familiar," I and Amy said together. But neither of us figures out whose.

"So our mission is to find what's in the archives," Lena asked. "Exactly," I said, and all of us started to check every one of them.

"For Ava, Max, Laura…" Amy paused for a second. "Girls," She said, and then pointed out the next letter in her hands. *For Chloe.*

CHAPTER 12

January 9th, 4:34 pm

After school we headed straight to the seashore. Jack was standing there, the same as the night we saw him. He stared at the ocean as if searching for answers in the deep abyss.

"Hey!" Elle called him from behind. "Staring won't help, if only we could get the answers from the depths of this wide ocean, I would wish it were a little less deep; the deeper you go, the tighter the tangled truth will be". She took a deep breath, sighing at the endless sea. "I am doing this for my sisters, but why, why would one swim deeper if they can feel how tight the trap is? Aren't you a detective? Can I ask you why?"

Jack glanced at Elisa, then he turned his gaze to me. "Because, the more you feel suffocated, the more you will wish to live, the more the questions are, the more eager you will swim towards the answers, am I right, Emma? Or should I call you Jr. Austin?" The way he said that made me feel like the tides in the ocean were getting louder and louder, like they echoed his words, my father's words. "The deeper the mysteries are, the more you will crave for the answers."

My father knew my father. A sudden wave of wind brought me back to that day. Lights. Ambulances. The sky became darker. My eyes became blurry.

***

"Em! Em!" As I opened my eyes, everyone was around me. I was at home, and Jack was there too. Drops of water sprinkled on my face. My head ached as if I had hit my head on a rock. My eyes pointed at the clock in the middle of the dining hall. It was 6 in the evening. I was unconscious for two hours. I stood up from the couch. "What... really happened? Did I faint?"

"You fainted on the seashore, we couldn't wake you up, we guess it was the aftereffect," Elle told me. "After effect? Of what? Should I bring you to the hospital?" Jack was confused. "Not necessary, it is not the first time I have fainted because of my past. Every time I hear something about my past that triggers my memories, I will faint for some hours, but I will be fine. We have gone to hospitals many times. It is no use," I told him. "Oh, right, how do you know my father? How can you know his words? Were you one of his colleagues?"

"Not really, years before you were born, your father was one of the best policemen in the city, he was my senior, he used to say those words to every newcomer. I was also a newcomer at that time. But because of unknown reasons, your father quit his job, so did Mr. Benjamin, Samuel, and

William. I haven't heard of them since then. I didn't get a chance to repay his kindness at that time, now I think that's why you girls appeared in front of me. Since you are really into this case, I will help you. But you have to promise me not to act on your own. Got it?"

At last, he agreed. "And now," Jack sat at the very end of the couch, "We can discuss the case".

Amy started the discussion, which was about the group we had learned about. "Well, Nora and Chloe had two best friends, Sarah and Claire, and the four were known as the pride of our school. But the year before we joined this school, something that had a great influence on them happened. Although we are not clear about what it is, the four were torn apart after that, teachers changed their classes, and they never seemed to be the same 'best friends' that they were before. People never again saw them interacting with each other."

"Then… did you try talking to those two? Sarah and Claire," Jack asked. "Ah, that is how we ended up getting a detention," Elle told him.

"And we got some new news, some letters." I took out the letter from my bag, not the one I received.

"We got it from our school letter Archive. We have a letter service, one can write to another through this, and if they are not valuable, one can dispose of the letters in the archives when finished reading. The letters will be burned every week," I said, handing him the letter.

To,

Chloe Fernandez

Hope you remember Ally, Ally Maxine, or do you? Maybe you have forgotten, but I haven't, I can't. Nor will I let you. I'm going to make you pay Chloe! Make you regret every decision you have taken, you will have the same fate as Nora. You will pay for what you have done wrong. If you don't want anything to come out, meet me at the Meraine Seashore tonight.

"This, this is a vital clue, you told me that letters get burned every one week, right? So there is a chance this was written the night Chloe died, and it may be the murderer who wrote this.

This is really helpful. I'll take care of the rest. You all go get some sleep. Then I shall go now, it is getting darker, I know you all are on your own, so remember to lock all the doors and windows, we can't be sure who he is targeting next." He left with a warning.

The handwriting of that letter, and that of the letter that I received first, is the same; it is the same person who wrote it. And who is Ally Maxine? What does she have to do with these?

I went upstairs, to the balcony, the same place as ever, to stare at the moon. I sighed, glancing at the sky. Even though things that are happening lately aren't friendly enough, there was still the same old breeze to coax me.

I walked into my room, looking through every corner I could reach; the same butterfly was there; it was on top of one of my books.

That was the only time I realized something was out of order; that book wasn't supposed to be there, it was out of order. The moment I realized that something was off, I had the same headache. My eyes got blurry, through a peek, I could see the butterfly was not there anymore, but before I could react, I fell into my bed.

CHAPTER 13

January 10th, 6:34 am

The next morning, the sun shone through the curtains and pierced my eyes. The wind was blowing unusually strongly. It was January 10th. The day that I have forgotten. The day our parents died. I could hear someone's steps, climbing the stairs, it was in a panicky motion, the speed got higher, and I found the person yelling my name. It was Elle. I opened the door, and it was not just Elle; everyone was there.

"Claire… Claire is murdered." That sentence echoed in my mind a thousand times. "When? Where?" I was confused. "Another seashore, last night, and Sarah was kidnapped". A gut feeling told me that I was right, and it was yesterday when the butterfly last came. I couldn't possibly find a logical explanation for this.

But how was it possible that it was not his style? This time, it felt like he was in a rush. But why? Maybe he knew we found out about them, but how? Amy got a notification.

It was from Jack. He told us to meet him at his house. Everything was upside down. Another notification, from the school group, states that the school is closed because of the chaos out there. Students are advised not to leave their houses unless it is an emergency.

"Maybe they're afraid that the killer won't stop here," Lena said, reading the message from the group. "I don't think so," I said, "I think it is the end. We couldn't do anything but watch. The killings are going to end, my mind says, clearly, the killer was targeting that group, and the ones that remained were Sarah and Claire. Now they are also captured; there is nothing we can do now. But it is clear now, whatever the heck that happened with their group, has something to do with their death".

***

We got ready to go to Jack's place; he might have figured out something. It was far away from our house. A 30-minute ride. It was not a big apartment, just enough for one person to live. We knocked on the door. Jack opened the door, and his face was not pleasant. He took a look around the courtyard, then said, "Come in".

The walls were filled with the details of the cases he had ever dealt with. There were many unfinished ones. "If I am right, you thought someone was tailing us and you looked around just now to ensure no one was behind us, right?" I said, looking around the cases on the wall. "You sure are quite observant, the killer knew the second we thought those two students were suspicious, that's why he rushed this time, and if I am right, the killer is someone close to us or is someone who is following me or you all," He said, while pouring water for us.

"Think carefully, if you have come across anyone you think is suspicious, or have you ever thought something is off?" He asked me, giving me a glass of water. Something came to my mind last night, Butterfly, the *book*. Without saying a word, I left the place, rushing towards our house. Elle and others followed me. The book, why didn't I think of it?

I reached home, climbing the stairs as fast as I could. I rushed to my room, and the book was still there. I went through the pages. Others were clueless about my strange behavior. At last, I found a piece of paper with a number written on it.

I grabbed my phone and dialed that number. Someone picked up that it was a familiar voice, but I just couldn't recall where I had heard it. I put the phone on speaker.

"Emma, you sure are as observant as your mother. You noticed the small change in the order of the books I made, but you were a little late. I thought you could be a little more… quick. But you still have time. Do you remember the game your father taught you? A thing is hidden somewhere, you have to find it within the small time, with the help of the clues, here let's play the game again, the culprit is now on the abandoned building on the western seashore, if you can make it before 30 minutes, maybe you can find out who the culprit is, remember, time is limited" saying this, the call ended. I couldn't call back.

How could he know what happened in my childhood? How can he know the game my father taught me? How does he know where the culprit is? Is he the killer? How… did he know my name?

Everything was out of order since this case showed up. I have been reminded of my parents over and over. What actually did happen on January 10th? Is it a mere coincidence that today is 10th January? But in this state, coincidences don't even exist.

CHAPTER 14

January 10th, 8:02 am

I rushed to the western seashore. Elle and others notified Jack about the situation. I have never been this fast ever. Right when I reached the seashore, I saw a person in black running towards the abandoned building. The person started to run as soon as he saw me. I followed. We reached the top of the building. The person removed the cap. It was a lady. She wore a mask.

"I never thought you would find me, Emma." That was a familiar voice. A very familiar voice.

"Teacher?" I said, wishing it would be someone else. But no. She removed her mask. It was my mathematics teacher, Alice.

"So that is why you knew what we were doing, but why? Why would you do such things? I'm mistaken, right? You are not the culprit, are you?" My voice broke down when I said it. But now that I was sure of it, the handwriting is hers. I'm sure that was how we were familiar with the handwriting.

"I am the one you are searching for. I killed them," She said. Those words were firm enough to let me know how much she hated them, but why? I wish it were a dream, I wish I'm hallucinating, but every inch in my body said it was real, the person I was looking for is in front of me.

"Why would you do it!" I yelled at her with all my strength. Tears filled my eyes.

"I know why," Another voice jumped into the air. Jack was here. "Years ago, a girl named Ally was found dead on this same seashore. The case was considered a suicide until some witnesses came in. They were Sarah, Claire, Chloe, and Nora. The police saw in some of the CCTV that they also headed to the seashore at the same time. The witnesses said they saw someone pushing Ally from this building. But the case was still unsolved as they failed to find who the culprit is. Ally had only one relative, her sister, *Alice*." That was another stab in my body.

He continued, "But her sister Alice firmly believed that the witnesses were the ones who killed her sister, as they didn't get along so well at their school."

Hearing this, Alice shouted, "Weren't I right? They are the only ones who saw my Ally that day, and why do you think a little girl would go to an abandoned building at night? That night, she told me she was going to get rid of her misfortune. She said that as if she were going to be reborn. I had never seen her that happy since she transferred to this school. Every night, I could hear her silently crying in her room, that night… she sneaked out of the house late at night. I didn't notice it till her room was strangely silent. I went to her room, only to find her bed empty. I searched all over her room, and that is when I got her diary. She had written all her sufferings in her diary, the last sentence in was, 'If it weren't for those four, I wouldn't be here anymore.' The rest was torn away. My Ally died because of them." She added a pause to her part of the story.

I felt extremely helpless. I hate her for being heartless, she used be a motherly figure for us, she was second to our Aunt. We grew up without our parents; it was our Aunt. There was only our Aunt to take care of us until we moved into this city, and Alice was the best mentor I have ever had. Apart from the moon, the second one I shared my burden with.

I can't blame her for loving her sister with all her heart. Those students deserved punishment, but from the law, if it's death, then it should be a death sentence, not a murder.

"Where the hell is Sarah?" Jack asked her behind me, "Alice, we can understand your situation, but ruining one's life doesn't make you different from those girls. Now, please, where is Sarah?"

She smirked, "My emotions are buried within my sister's grave, Jack. I know you are a good human and a great detective, but let me make you understand how failing as both feels like, even if you search for her your entire life, you won't find her." Her words were stern.

“You weren't a bad human nor a terrible sister; the situations made you,” Jack said, but I knew it was just for calming her down

“What I am is my choice, no one makes me anything.”

“Then why did you leave a message for us? Where is my family photo? Why did you send a letter to me?” I asked, and that question seemed to have confused her. “I don't know about your family picture or whatsoever, nor have I messaged you,” She said out of the blue. I knew it was not her.

“But can you make sure that you know the whole story, Miss Alice?” That was crimson. How did she get here? No Idea. “You told them that you saw her diary. Tell me what you saw? Huh? Tell me which sentence in that diary said they were the bullies? Tell me!! Oh Lord, if I knew you were her sister, I would have begged your forgiveness, but not because I killed, because I failed to protect her!” She began to be more aggressive. I have never seen her like this, never.

“You told them the story from your perspective, now let me tell you mine. What you know is that the four were the bully gang, but did you know there was a fifth one? It was *me*, did you think there was a sixth one? It was your sister Alice!” She paused.

I could see through things not clearly but a little blurry, it was Crimson who told us about their group, it was her who triggered the things in our mind for us to connect the dots, from the beginning till the end she was there, At the mourning ceremony, she was there when we discussed about them, or it was her who gave us the clues about them, from the starting point, *it was her*.

These things flashed through my mind as she continued, "But it was not some kind of bully gang; we were victims, the school bully gang used to bully us, as the common victims, we became friends. One day, we decided not to be their victims anymore, we recorded the videos of them bulling us, at that night, we decided to meet up to discuss what we should do further, but Ally, she arrived earlier than us, I used another route to get there, so that my parents wouldn't notice much, but because of that, I weren't caught on cameras. But when I arrived, Sarah, Claire, Nora, and Chloe were hiding behind a wall. We saw a man in black, pushing Ally from here; we could do nothing. I hid behind one of the pillars. We were helpless.

After that man left, we rushed downstairs, only to find Ally covered in blood. I got a piece of paper from her hands; she had held it so strongly that it was the rest of the page from her diary. I kept it till now," she handed the paper to me.

I am so grateful that they are here. If I were to endure it alone, I would have died by now. Now that we have the evidence, we can finally be free from those monsters. What I only have left as good memories in this year are the moments with them. I hope we can be friends forever.

Those were her last words; she wrote from her heart, she might have wanted a normal life like others, with her friends. She might have wanted them to be happier than she was, but the result of unspoken words was huge misunderstandings. Now they are dead, because of her sister; they've been wronged thoroughly.

Crimson continued, "As the witness, I was not brave enough to stand up for her, and I regret it all my life, but them… they were the only ones who stood up for her, if not for them, this case wouldn't have even been considered as murder, but what did they get in return? *They died*, Alice, they died! in front of you…" She burst out in sadness, she was crying, louder than ever.

"From the second I knew Chloe and Nora had been murdered, I warned Emma and others with the information I got. I was sure they would find something, but… if I knew it was you." She leaned to the pillar behind her.

"So you were the one who messaged us?" I suddenly asked her.

"You also got a message? Someone messaged me also, but I don't know who." Her voice was cracking as she spoke to me. She was crying nonstop.

I wanted to do so too, but I couldn't; it was like my tears refused to. I stood there, mesmerized. Was it because of me? From my childhood till now, the people around me have suffered. I can't socialize much, but the ones I trust have all left me, or are suffering because of me, my parents, my friends, and now my teacher. Alice began to murmur something, but my world became silent; I couldn't hear a single thing. As I stood there, my mind became blank, and I heard a sudden scream, Jack rushing to the end of the building, *Alice jumped*. I felt like something pushed me from behind, like it was a stone. I fainted.

I could hear the sounds of ambulances and police vehicles. Behind me, Elle was on a phone call with Aunt Ethal. I could hear her yelling, "How many times should I tell you girls to get out of trouble, huh? What do you think you are? Super detectives!? You girls are all over the internet, *'students who caught the culprit; is police not capable?'* she read the headlines out loud.

Elle was trying her best to calm her down. After all the chaos, I'm still there. I don't know how many people there are left for me to lose; still, I am obligated to inhale oxygen. Tell me, why does it feel like a punishment? The only thing that makes me accept the punishment is an unknown hope.

PART TWO

CHAPTER 15

March 19, 9:48 am

After that incident, we decided to live apart from Aunt. We moved to the new city, and after all this chaos, we lost contact with most of the people from our last city. The last time we went there was for exams and, of course, for graduation. I don't know how much time passed by like that. Roughly 2 months. Yes, it has been two months since my mouth refused to speak. Well, till last week, I spoke again. But it didn't make me happy. I wasn't, I am not till now, but now I have to force a smile for a college interview.

We all got ready. But the problem was that the interview was at 10 and now it is 9:50. I spent my whole morning trying to tie a tie and ended up choosing a dress to wear rather than a suit, I mean, it's not like I am getting a job. We all rushed to get a taxi. We had bought a car, but since it was needed by our neighbor, we didn't have a choice.

I was almost jumping in front of the taxis. At last, we got one.

We were late, but fortunately, it was not our turn yet. I walked into the room where other students were sitting. They called my name as soon as I entered, '*Emma Elizabeth Austin*' which felt like a death call. I didn't even have the chance to sit down. Sweat running down, my heartbeats getting faster and faster. I walked into the interview room, and there were five people in the room, and oh, they looked like they were going to kill me. It was an AC room, yet I was sweating. They asked me a question I never knew I was able to answer, but there I am, walking out of the room. Everyone was staring at me. After me, my friends were called one by one.

'Elisa William Dormen'

'Amy Sarah Benjamin'

'Lena Elsa Samuel'

The interview wasn't hard enough that I would fail the interview, and I don't mean to brag, but it was already a sure thing with my marks. We couldn't take a taxi from the college, so we had to walk down the streets to take a taxi. There was a stressful silence between us.

"How about getting some ice cream?" I said, breaking the silence between us. "That would be awesome," Lena said.

We were right in front of an ice cream shop. As we sat at the shop, we went back to the time we were truly happy, the time we lived with our parents. I saw myself in the mirror of the ice cream shop, talking to my mother. "Mommy! What does this pendant mean?" I asked my mother, who was reading a book, I cannot recall which one. "It's a snowflake, it is said that snowflake symbolizes purity and hope, if you like it, then I will give it to you," She said, giving me the necklace, and I still have it with me, still after 10 years. I didn't know it would last this much.

Amy also remembered some things from our childhood: "Remember my 9th birthday? My dad got me a talking teddy as a birthday gift, that night we fought for the teddy," She exclaimed.

It was her 9th birthday; Uncle Ben bought her a talking teddy which repeatedly said 'HAPPY BIRTHDAY AMY!'. We were all jealous to see that gift; it was our first time seeing one. That night, we did a pillow fight to see who could win the talking teddy. Seeing this, my mother brought us three other talking teddies the next morning.

We didn't notice that our ice cream was melting. I went to the counter to pay, and that was when I saw a lady staring at our table. Maybe I was just overthinking, but even though she wore a mask preventing me from seeing her face, she, she is extremely *familiar*. I wasn't sure where or when.

I diverted my attention to the counter. Right when I was going to pay, Amy wanted another ice cream. She told me and was going to get one, but that lady came to us. "I am so sorry to ask, but do you have a 20 to spare? I am not sure if I can return it or not," she asked. I gave it to her even though that was the only $20 I had left; Amy couldn't buy another ice cream.

But all that mattered to me was that her voice was similar, similar to that of my mother's. I was completely disturbed. Even when in the taxi, to go back home, I was thinking, if it was just my thoughts, when I saw her, I saw that she hadn't ordered much, but still she had to borrow another 20 to pay her bill. I don't know what I am thinking, or what I am expecting her to be. I don't, but I can't help but think about it.

We reached home in seconds, or I didn't notice seconds become minutes because I was immersed in thoughts. Our car had been returned. We walked up the stairs to our apartment. I couldn't keep it to myself, so I told others. "Amy, don't you think that the lady who came to us was a bit weird? Or in some way, her voice was familiar, familiar that of my mother's. Elle stopped walking when she heard a strange lady's sound similar to that of my mother's.

"What do you mean by that, Em? So what? It's been years since you've heard Aunt Amanda's voice. How can you be so sure that it was hers? Or what if it is similar? What does it change? Does it change the fact that she's dead? Does it change the fact that they all left us alone? So please stop picking up old memories that don't matter." She is sensitive when it comes to that incident, I mean, it was not just me who lost her parents, they did too, she did too. And she fought, a lot harder than we all, she was the oldest among us, so when our parents left us, she was more responsible whenever Aunt wasn't around.

When our parents died, I had a hard time remembering the things that happened that day. The doctor said that my mental condition also affected my physical condition. We had to skip school for one year, and we didn't finish the year we were in, so that made us waste our two years. Since my parents died, Aunt had to take on part-time jobs, she would work overtime and finish her studies at the same time. When she was not home, Elle was the one who took care of us. Sometimes she had to even cook for us.

I still remember one day, two months ago, we moved on from that city where we lived with our parents. It was a Sunday, Aunt left us at noon, saying she would come back before evening, but she didn't. She didn't come back even after 9 pm. We didn't even have lunch.

Elle knew we were starving; moreover, she hadn't eaten either. She went to the kitchen, she was only 10, and she couldn't even reach the shelf. She took a vessel, filled it with water and put it in the stove, had a little bit trouble with turning it on, I thought the house was going to explode the next second, but luckily it didn't.

But when she tried to open the lid, the boiling water fell onto her hand, she screamed with pain, her hand was severely burned, but she still put the vessel back onto the stove. She made some noodles, which were not perfect, but all we needed to fill our stomachs. We didn't know how to treat her burn, little did she.

It was 11 pm when Aunt came home. She apologized for being late and then saw the burn on Elle's hand. She was so panicked and immediately treated her burn. I still remember how helpless she looked on that day; she could neither leave us alone again nor leave her job to look after us. Elle was so frustrated that day, about her parents, she believed that if they didn't leave us back then Aunt wouldn't have had to endure all this, she had always blamed her parents, how much she had wanted to wake up one day and see that all of that were just a dream, but every morning we woke up to bitter reality. She still has that mark on her hand; it never disappeared. She would wear long-sleeve tops to avoid letting others see it. Even in the summer, she would wear long-sleeved clothes, but I know for her it wasn't the mark that mattered; every time she sees that mark, it reminds her of the pitiful life we once had.

A wish bloomed in my mind as I thought about my mother. I wanted to see her, not just my mother, but all others. Since we moved from the city where they were buried, we have never visited them. "I... I want to see them," I said when we were about to enter the house.

"Emma, it's a five-hour drive from here to there; it would take more than 11 hours for us to get back here, and it's already noon," Amy told me.

"Let her, Amy, after all, it's been over a decade since we last visited," Elle said. So we didn't bother to enter the house, we left right away for our hometown.

Elle was the one who was driving. Lena was the passenger queen, Amy, and I sat on the back seats. Time passed like minutes. I could see my old town; it had changed a lot. The big old buildings where there used to be a grand restaurant, a playground which remained the same, and oh, our school, which is practically the same but did have some renovations. I recalled the time I was here, not the gloomy me, the shiny me, with my friends, of course, at that time we used to fool kids in our class, saying we were siblings. They thought Lena and I were non-identical twins. I didn't make that up, but as they did, we didn't bother explaining. Where are they now? Even though I don't remember the names of most of them, I still want to meet them again, for once.

We reached the graveyard, and it was still the same. I think it was the church people who kept it the same. And there were bouquets in front of all of them. But all other graves had red roses, except that of Aunt Emily and Uncle William; those were white roses. We sat down talking to our parents after years. Everything we have ever achieved. For the first time, I saw Elle crying, even when she had to endure so much pressure. Growing up, I had rarely seen her crying. She was yelling loudly at her parents. No one stopped her. She cried until she wanted to.

Remembering every phase of life, we were like migrating birds, we were born in our parents' hometown, but after the youngest one, I was born, we moved to this city where we lived till our parents died, two months after that accident we moved to another city, from where we gradually moved again because of some problems I had to meet with while on school, then we moved to the last city with Aunt Ethal, from where we moved to our current place after the Alice event. I went over to console her. We decided to leave the place because we were getting too emotional.

I stepped on one of the bouquets laid on the grave of Elle's parents, and then a note slipped from it. *'To the most loving people,'* that was the note in it. I don't know why, but I kept the note. We walked towards our cars. We didn't stay any longer because it was already late. Elle was the one who drove a bit from the city, but she had shown all her frustration with driving, so eventually Lena took over driving.

We reached our home by 12 am. And I was sure that going on a ten-hour trip to my old hometown after an exhausting interview was not a good idea. We parked our car and then walked towards our apartment, but then we heard screaming from the other side of the wall. We went to see what was happening. A man was being robbed by a group of gangsters.

Lena shouted from behind, "Hey, you losers! Don't you feel ashamed of being a five-member gang to beat up one single man?" That was when they noticed us; they immediately ran away when they saw us. We went over to look who the person was. He looked severely injured. I leaned down to ask him if he was okay. I mean, he clearly wasn't okay. That was when I saw his face. "It's you!" I said, looking at the man that I saw at the library.

"You know each other?" Elle asked me. "Well, yeah, kinda," then I turned to him, "Will, right?"

"Hey, Hazel! And yes, Will for William, thank you for today, and for remembering the name," He said, trying to stand up. He could barely do that. "Do you need to go to the hospital?" Amy asked, helping him stand up. "Well, I would've if they didn't run away with my bag, which had my wallet," He said as if it wasn't a big deal. "Where do you live?" I asked out of the sudden, "I saw you in our city back then, why are you here?"

"I live in this city. That day, I came to that city to meet someone, and I was moving out of my last place. I rented out an apartment here, but I lost my way while coming here, so I got late, and I just got here and was planning to move my stuff up when I came across those gangsters," he said, pointing at the boxes at the corner. "And what about you? Here for college? And by the way, did you find the butterfly?" He asked.

"Well, yeah, yes, we are here for college, and no, I didn't find the butterfly, but I solved the Rubik's cube!" I replied. Lena and others were staring at me, wondering what butterfly and Rubik's cube I was talking about.

"Well, how about we help you move your things? You are really injured in the first place," Lena asked him. "If you don't mind, yes," He said.

And that was it, after a 10-hour drive, I was waiting to fall onto my bed, but all of a sudden, I had to move things from here to there. I am so going to break my back.

"What a great idea of yours!" I told Lena. "Why are you upset about it? Isn't he your friend? Friends help each other, and my friend's friend is also my friend," She replied, lifting one comparatively smaller box from there. "Correction, we've only met once, and that doesn't make us friends, and yeah, if you feel like helping, do it yourself! Why drag us into it?" I said, putting another box on top of the box she was holding.

Fortunately, there were not so many boxes. We climbed up the stairs as he led the way; his apartment was on the 2nd floor. I thanked god that it was not on the 5th floor. The elevator was out of order, so we had to use the stairs. We put down the things in front of his apartment, waiting for him to open the door. "Oh no," He said, checking his pockets. "They had my keys too! Looks like I have to wait till the locksmith comes," He said, staring at the closed door. When

I looked behind, they all had escaped pretty fast. Lena looked behind while running, "Help him move the stuff, we're tired!" She shouted and then ran to our apartment. Great! Now I am stuck with an injured man and a bunch of boxes.

"I never told you my name. I am Emma," I turned to him. "I am sorry for this. I hope the locksmith will arrive soon," He said. I looked around. Every other person was sleeping soundly. I was supposed to, too. "So how about chatting so that time doesn't count?" He leaned against one wall. "About what?" I sat down, moving the boxes. "Maybe about the butterfly, what was it for?" He asked, and that was a great topic to start with. Can I tell him that a weird butterfly appears in my room every time someone gets murdered? "For a school project," I came up with the most possible lie.

And that conversation went on for a long time. I don't remember how long until the locksmith arrived. We moved the stuff to his apartment. His wounds had stopped bleeding. "I would recommend sanitizing those wounds," I said, moving the last box. "I will," He said.

I didn't linger much longer there. I climbed up the stairs to our apartment, which was on the 3rd floor. The first thing I did as soon as I entered was to throw my slippers somewhere and run into my room. Lena had made my room a mess with the excuse that she was trying to borrow one of my clothes. All the clothes she had tried on were still left untouched in the bed. I did not bother to clean the mess. I just slept on top of the clothes. But before I closed my eyes, I could see the magical butterfly lingering in my room. This time I had a close look at it, magical it is, with pink and purple on its wings. I don't know how I fell asleep.

CHAPTER 16

March 19, 9:48 am

I got a notification in the morning. It was from the college where we had gone for the interview. We passed! I ran to the living room to tell everyone the news. Lena was jumping in the air. "We have to celebrate," She said, looking at me. "Not my treat, I treated you girls just yesterday!" I said, knowing her look meant that I had to pay. "Then let it be my treat," Elle said. "At least I don't have to cook today. When will you girls ever learn to cook?" She asked.

We went to the same ice cream shop as yesterday. "I had expected a five-star restaurant with expensive side dishes!" Lena whispered. "Yeah, unless Elle has won a lottery ticket," Amy said, mocking Lena.

Despite of not letting her go to a restaurant, Lena had bought the most expensive ice cream in the shop. We bought the same as yesterday. I went to get the bill with Elle's card.

The man at the counter was not the same one as yesterday. I paid the bill and bought one packet as a parcel.

We walked through the streets after her treat. Amy looked at the ice cream I had bought. "Why didn't you buy the chocolate ice cream flavor? And why do you have two bills?" She asked.

"Two bills?" No, there's no two bills – As I looked through the cover, there were indeed two papers, one was the bill, and the other? I picked up the other paper, and everyone looked curiously at it. It had my name on it, 'To Emma,' it said. I opened the folded paper *'It doesn't end with Alice, it won't end, and you can't run away, neither can your friends. This game involves five of you, and starts with the five of you. It depends on you if the game ends with the same five; it will all end when you remember what you forgot.*

That was what it had said. If I am right, it might be the same person who had called me that day Alice died, the one who stole my photo, the one who sent me letters about the archive. Elle grabbed that piece of paper and ripped it into pieces. "You are *not* going after this. We have had enough trouble for the last few months," She said, throwing those pieces in the streets.

"But it said that none of us can escape until she remembers," Amy said nervously. "It's utter nonsense! Do you think this psych can make her do what the experienced doctors failed to do? And what is with the five of us? We are four!" Elle yelled, "Now, this is just another insane person who may have seen the news about us from years ago; this doesn't mean we have to go behind every single note like this." She burst out with anger. This was not the first time I had received notes like this, after my parents died. Some freaks at school had given me notes like this. But this time it was entirely different in some ways, I mean, who remembers a case from 10 years ago? And I don't think it had mistakenly said five, it had something that caught my mind, and the butterfly, I think it has appeared every time something bad happens in my life. But what have I forgotten? What is this someone after? I want to know, though Elle has said so, I want to, I have to.

CHAPTER 17

March 20th, 10:23 am

I was sitting on the couch when I heard a doorbell. I went over to open the door. It was William. "Hey, Hazel," He said with an awkward look, still hasn't changed my name, I guess. "Hey, and what brings you here?" I asked.

"Can I come in?" He asked, and I let him in. Lena was with her face mask on, which almost scared the hell out of him.

"Nice to meet you again, Em's soon-to-be friend," she said, taking off the face mask. "Lena!" I pinched her. "What? You said he's not your friend, but this is how you make friends, so he is a soon-to-be friend!" Oh, she has absolutely lost her mind.

Elle moved the clothes on the couch, murmuring, "Goodness, why should he come exactly when this house is an absolute mess!"

"How are your wounds?" I asked, pouring a glass of water. "Much better, and both thank you and sorry for yesterday," He said. "Yeah, it was my pleasure helping someone except for the fact that I had to sleep at 3 and wake up at 8" I replied, handing him the glass of water. "So are you just here to thank me?"

"No, okay, so I know it might sound a little absurd, maybe a lot, but I received an envelope this morning and I think I should show you," He said, taking out an envelope from his pocket.

I took the envelope and started to read it.

But the only mistake you made was to show up in my game uninvited. Now that you are in, try not to be dead at the end. At least you deserve to be here, I suppose you know your team mates, find Emma to know more about this.

But I noticed, the top part of the envelope was torn apart, the part with the addressing, the part that I am reading now feels like it's from the middle of a conversation. "Where is the rest?" I asked, looking at the envelope. "I don't know, it came like this," He said.

Amy stared at Elle as she saw what was in it. "Okay, so that was what they meant by five of us," She said. "Who are they?" He asked, confused. "We also received a note this morning when we went to buy ice cream," I told him

"So where is that now?" He asked. We all stared at Elle. "Okay, I thought it was just another note from an insane person, who knew someone else would get the note too."

Now it was more than a piece of paper with a bunch of nonsense in it. He knows us very well, knows about our parents, what's more, he even knows about a person that we just met. What does he mean by him being deserving to be in this so-called game? I mean, what *is* this game?

CHAPTER 18

March 20, 9:05 pm

I waited to see the butterfly. If it only appears when some crazy things happen, it has to come now. Like I had expected, about 9 pm, it entered my room through the window. This time, I tried to catch the butterfly. I didn't know what I was thinking. When everything around you is turning upside down, nothing logical catches my eye. It flew around my room. I was running around to catch that freaking thing.

It at last rested upon my pillow. It was glowing. I removed my pillow. There it was, a note, again. This time, it had said 'Specifically for Ms. Austin.' I opened the note; this time it was a long one.

Greetings, Emma Elizabeth Austin

First of all, sorry for starting the game without an introduction. I thought you might end up being the next victims of your beloved teacher. But you were smart, colluding with that detective. I didn't know you would be so into the game that you thought you started because you wanted to, but no, you didn't have a choice in the first place. But congratulations on completing the first half successfully. Now it's time for the second half. I got an uninvited guest, too. I guess you have met him. He thought he was smart, but he ended up showing himself to me, or else I wouldn't have known of his existence. Don't try to ignore things around you; they will only get you deeper into this game. And one kind of advice, don't trust the people around you so easily, maybe they turn out to be lying about who they are, don't tell me I didn't warn ya!

Best wishes on your next game,

Hunter

That was it, Hunter. I don't know what he meant by that. I don't know what he meant by anything he has written. The butterfly vanished, and I was left with the letter. I heard knocks on my room door. It was Elle and others. Turns out that they have also received letters.

"What does this all mean?" Amy asked, holding the letters. I opened all of them one after one.

Greetings, Amy Sarah Benjamin

Oh, that name reminds me of your parents, those brats. They hid the fact that you all existed, and they thought they could hide it forever. But look now, they may be seeing this from heaven. They tried to escape the game, and they died. Now the game has selected you and your fellow friends. Try to keep yourself safe. Don't be stupid like your parents. But if it comes to a point that your friends should choose themselves or you, who would you think they would choose? The second round will start soon……

Hunter

Greetings, Elisa William Dormen

How was the first round? Had fun? Don't worry, the next round is starting too; this time, there is a little surprise waiting for you. Don't get too anxious. The Dormen family had always been brave, but what happened to you? Now that the descendants of Dormen have weakened into two, but surely you won't let your family down, right?

Hunter

Greetings, Lena Elsa Samuel

Hey! The brave one, huh? Well, let's hope you will remain as you are now. The next round is starting soon. And one reminder, keep a watch on your Aunt, maybe one holds much more than you do. You think that you know everyone better, you think that you are strong, but are you?

Hunter

I completed reading. "Every letter had one common factor, it repeatedly said about the next round. According to this so-called hunter, Alice was the first round of his game. So does it mean another round of killings is going to happen, and Elle, in your letter, he said two descendants, but you are the only descendant of your family, right?" I said.

Suddenly, as I put down her letter on my table, the glass of water that I had put next to my table fell down, and the letter got wet, completely wet. We couldn't dry the letter; the ink had spread all over.

"Em," Elle called my name. "We all have received letters, and if I am right, William is also a part of this, so does it mean that he has also received one?" What she said made sense, so we went to his apartment. I knocked on the door. He opened in minutes. He invited us in. "What happened?" He asked, rubbing his eyes. "Um, nothing, it's just have you received any strange letters?" I asked.

"Yeah, the one I got this morning," He said. "No, not the one you received this morning, like under your pillow or something? We all received one," I said.

"No, I didn't," He replied, "But can I see the letters you all received?" I handed him the letters. "Feel free to sit," he said, pointing at the dining table. We sat down. I could see his face changing when he was reading my letter. But it was as if he hid that expression of his. When I knocked at his door, he looked like he was just out of bed, but how did he open the door so fast? I remembered the words in the letter. *Don't trust*. He had completed reading the letters.

"Where is yours?" He asked Elle. "We got it wet by accident," Elle replied. "Emma, can you tell me what the content of the letter was?" He asked me.

"I only read the letter once, but it mentioned her family. He said that her family was the bravest, but that she wasn't the same as her family. The letter ended by telling her not to let down her family," I said, but I didn't mention the descendants thing.

He sighed, then started speaking, "Emma, do you have a problem with trusting people?" He asked me, which had got me thinking, it made my mind go blank, yes, I had, I don't trust people, I want to, every time I trust someone, they end up hiding things from me, my parents, Crimson, Alice. I didn't answer his question. "I suppose your silence is a yes." Then he turned to Amy, "Amy, what about you? Do you think you are weak? Do you think that you rely too much? Do you think you are not brave? Do you see yourself as a burden to your friends?" That was it, he was purposefully poking at our weak points.

"What do you mean, William? Are you trying to make us feel bad? You asked me if I don't trust people or not, then hear me out, I don't, and you are the number one in that list, a stranger turning out be living as the same apartment as us, and you are in the strange game that we are in too, you have not received letters when we all did, and you made it look like you came out from your bed but then how did you answer the door in seconds, how can we believe a stranger that popped up in our life isn't the hunter, what if you are the hunter?" I burst out. He said nothing, then smiled.

"It's okay if you don't trust me, or that's what this 'hunter' wants you to do. He has been manipulating all of you. When reading the letters, he purposefully added your weaknesses or your insecurities, for you it was you trust issues, for Amy it was her inner thought that she is a burden to all of you that triggered when he asked her if she think you all will stand up for her forever, for Elisa I assume that she thinks that she can't protect you all well enough, she thinks she isn't capable enough as her parents, for Lena, he is using her loved ones to confuse her, for most of the people the people they wants to trust would be their family and friends, the same goes for her. He knows you all well."

He was right about everything. I apologized for shouting. "Then what should we do now? We were a part of the first round of this game, but you weren't. I assume you have heard of the Alice killings news; it was all over the internet. But he is saying that there is more. Does it mean there will be more of the killings?" I asked.

"Not necessarily, it can be anything, but since it involves me too, he might be aiming for something. What was in the first letter you all received? Did it mention anything particular?" He asked. There was. It was about my condition, he said it will only end if I remember what happened 10 years ago. But I didn't want to tell him about my parents, about the pitiful past. About me being a witness to my own parents' death. So I kept silent. He might have noticed it.

"It is fine if there is anything that you don't want me to know, but as teammates, we need to know each other. If you don't want to start, then I will. I am an orphan. My mother and father died in an accident, I don't really know them because I was two when this happened, I was left in an orphanage, but the only thing that reassured me was that I had an uncle, an Aunt and a cousin sister, they lived far away, but they would come and see me frequently, it was like I had another reason to live, I remember my sister, she was beautiful, a little soul who used to be like a sunshine in our orphanage, every time she visits, she would run around the play ground happily, I remember her name being Ellie. But I only remember her face till she was 4, after that, they stopped visiting. I thought they also had forgotten about me, but little did I know, they had died, like my mother did, they were also gone, four years after they last visited, they died. That is pretty much it, tragic, right? Do you think I am pitiful?"

He said as if it didn't really matter, but I could see it did, a lot. Every meeting we had had a pretentious look for me, but what he said right now wasn't a lie. No one can lie like that. "Not at all," I took a deep breath, "I don't think you are pitiful, we also lost our parents, we didn't have any other relatives other than Lena's Aunt, she wasn't blood related to any of us, but Lena, legally she didn't have any obligation to look after us, but she did.

Our parents died in a car accident when we were 8, on a January night, but the strangest fact was, when the police found the car, I was at the scene, they interrogated me, again and again, but the truth was, I don't remember, I don't remember a thing that happened that day. The note we received this morning said that this will only end when I remember what I had forgotten." I finished.

"Maybe this 'hunter' is somehow related to your parents and they are in desperate need to know what had happened that day, maybe someone really close to you but you don't remember" He said, I had thought that too, if to know us so well that they know about my memory, then they might be someone close to us or someone related to our parents but we have never noticed.

CHAPTER 19

March 20, 10:12 pm

I let my mind wander through the day after my parents had died. Most of the memories were of blurry and unfinished gaps; I don't remember much of it. It was completely normal; it had happened almost a decade ago.

But I remember lying on the grass, just near the highway where the accident happened. I felt helpless, I couldn't move, and just like that, that memory ended.

I was being taken to the hospital, soon after police found me, I recalled doctors asking me what my name was, where I lived, and who my parents were. I don't remember what I had told them, but not long after, Aunt rushed to the hospital with Elle, Amy, and Lena. They looked confused. Amy started crying as soon as she saw me lying in a hospital bed. There were police officers outside the room.

Then my mind went to some day later, I was still at the hospital, that day, the police officers had questioned me, a middle-aged man with his subordinate, whose face I don't recall, asked me whether I remembered the vehicle that hit my parents' car. That was the time I realized something was off. I was told by my Aunt that I was sick and that is why I was at the hospital. Really, I couldn't remember I was on the highway, and I thought I was really sick, which I was. But that was not the whole reason they took me to the hospital. I stared at Aunt, who was standing beside the police officer.

"I just told her that she had a fever," Aunt told the police officers.

"Aunt! What really happened to me? Why did they say my parents' car got hit?" I yelled, and tears were rolling down my cheeks. She hugged me tight and wiped the tears off my cheek. "Em, I'm sorry, and you need to know that I'm sorry, they had a car accident, 8 of them died." She was weeping too. I could see pain in her eyes as she comforted me, "But you were there, the police officers, they found you lying near the highway, you were unconscious. That is why you are in the hospital now. Em, can you recall anything that happened? Anything like how you got there?"

I was so helpless, for days after that, I strained myself to remember, it wasn't for the police. I needed to find out what had happened. They ran numerous tests on me. Scans after scans. But nothing was worth it. My brain was completely normal. But still, I couldn't remember a thing. The doctor who consulted me suggested that it might be a temporary memory loss, and that I shouldn't force myself to remember.

And just like that, they waited months for me to remember until the case was closed. It was a mere hit-and-run. But for me, it took the lives of my parents, as well as my friends' parents, ruined our lives, and made me a patient.

Now that I think of it, the truth about my memory loss wasn't flashed on TV channels. Neither did they know about it. We didn't tell anyone else. Aunt thought it might affect my daily life if it had been exposed. But my daily life became a little worse rather than a little better even after that.

But this 'hunter' knows. He clearly knows what happened to me. If the information wasn't disclosed to anyone else, then it would leave only a few candidates as the ones who know about my memory loss. I took out my notebook and started scribbling down:

Hunter- knows about my memory loss, behind Alice?

Memory loss, people who know: Elisa, Amy, Lena, Aunt Ethal, the doctor who consulted me, the middle-aged police officer, Natalia Sarah, my therapist from years ago.

The unknown message from two months ago- Hunter?

I looked at the list of people I remember knowing about my memory loss. I ruled out the first four; they can't be, of course, they are my family. And now what remains is three people, that police officer and doctor whom I don't know, and my therapist, Natalia.

And the only way I can look into these people is Aunt Ethal.

I heard someone knocking on my door. It was Elle. I opened the door. She was holding a glass of milk. "Here, it can help you get some sleep. I started to notice that you stay up almost the whole night these days." She placed the glass on my table. She saw the things I had written in my note. She picked it up and stared at me. "I want to know who this hunter is and why he is doing this," I said.

"Emma, I think we have talked about this. Just now, we found that this hunter knows more than he is supposed to know! He knows about us, you, and if this is not merely a prank but a psycho somewhere in the world trying to harm us, we are not supposed to dig up our own grave! Next morning, we will report this to the police, and no more excuses, you are *not* going after this mess like you did some months ago, you saw what it had resulted in, right?" Elle blew up and left the room.

I could hear her slamming the door of her room. I could understand her concern, but I can't just sit and watch as the police might or might not find this man, and just breathe knowing there is someone who can actually kill me the next second. From this, I've known, I can't persuade her, nor will she let Amy or Lena into this. Goodness.

CHAPTER 20

March 21, 4:57 am

This is my second time sneaking out without them noticing. But last time they had followed me all the way to the seashore, this time, I specifically checked that they were asleep. But I need a partner in crime.

I walked straight to Will's apartment and knocked. The first and second times, no one answered. The third time, I knocked too hard, so the lady next door was screaming, 'What is this fuss this early morning?' He did answer this time.

"Oh," He paused for a second, "What is it in this early morning, Hazel?"

"Just think that I am a morning person, quick, get your jacket on, and we have something to do, or at least *I* have," I said, letting myself into the apartment.

"And what would this mission be?" He asked, confused.

"Find that hunter and slap him in the face." I wrote it down in my notes as I told him.

We set off to my old city, where Aunt lives now. We barely visited her during our time in the new city; we could have used the weekends, but FaceTime two times a day felt enough.

I knocked on the door. Aunt opened the door with a bit of confusion. "Em!" She shouted right when she saw me. "Why didn't anyone tell me you were coming over? Where are the others? And who is this person beside you?" She asked, looking at William head to toe. She had asked too many questions at one time.

"Actually, I am here alone, and they are not with me. I didn't tell you in advance because I planned it five minutes before departing, and this is William, and I think I can address him as a friend, and also, *do not* tell Elisa that I came here," I answered her question all at once. We made our way to the living room.

"Where are we?" He whispered. "At my Aunt's house," I replied.

"And how is that related to the hunter?" He asked, sitting down on the couch beside me. I couldn't just say my whole night's thoughts in a few seconds without Aunt noticing, so I passed my note to him. "And why are you handing me a grocery lis–"

"Not that page!!" I shouted before Aunt could hear us. Aunt returned from the kitchen with a bowl of fruit. "Aunt, why do you look ten years younger than when I last visited you?" I was sugaring her up, and she knew.

"Oh dear, ten years ago I was nineteen, remember? And all that makes you tell me that I look like a reckless teenager is that you want a favor," She said, peeling an apple for me. William was still reading my note, trying really hard to understand my scribbles.

"Oh, who knows me better than you, right?" I gave her a sweet, nice, ever look. "Only if you had told me your needs that made you come to me, not only *without Elle noticing* and with a handsome fellow who seems confused about what the heck you are doing, and whatever it is, as I know Elle had disagreed, might be something reckless again," She replied, giving me the peeled apple.

"Oh well, now that you know, would you help me or not?"

"Can anything you are doing get you hurt?"

"No, Nope, and Never" *or maybe yes.*

"Well then, tell me, I will try to help you, but this is the last time I am helping you behind Elle's back." She agreed.

"So, I need the number of the therapist who used to consult me, as well as the doctor who consulted me after that incident happened, and also, do you remember who the police officer who was in charge of my parents' case?" I said all at once that it took her some time to understand, but I saw her face darkening as soon as she heard about my parents' case.

"Sweetie, would you mind telling me why you are interested in your parents' case that happened a decade ago? And why the therapist? Are you getting headaches again?" She asked me.

"Headaches?" William repeated after her. "Headache was a replacement word we used to mention my memory loss and its after effects, since we didn't want anyone else to know about it." I turned to him.

Aunt stared at William for a second, then told him that she wanted to talk with him alone, but obviously, I am going to eavesdrop. Aunt and William went to the kitchen.

"William, right?" William nodded as an answer

"Emma lost her parents at a very young age."

"I know," William cut her off in the middle. Maybe he didn't want to hear my tragic story once again.

"Good, I mean it's good that you know, but" There was a moment of silence. "Emma never let her mind forget the thing that happened to her parents, she wanted to remember, remember what happened that night, remember how she got there, even though she didn't have to; She firmly believed that something was really odd about that incident, it's true, finding her at the highway road was indeed odd, but that can't change the fact that they are gone, and digging into that too much had ruined her life as well.

If we think that way, we can say she is as reckless as Lena. There was a time when she used to get threatening notes from her school mailbox; she utterly believed that it was someone who was related to her parents' death. She even once called the police. But it turned out that it was just some random mean kids picking on an orphan kid. That had impacted her very much, since then, whenever she was reminded of her parents' death or about that night, she would get severe headaches or would instantly faint.

Only before two months ago, when a serial murder case was going on, her family picture got stolen, she glued to her assumption that it was the killer who had stole it, and he had something to do with her parents, but it turned out worse than she imagined, the serial killer turned out to be her teacher, and she had nothing to do with her family picture"

"Was that picture so important to her?"

"Of course, it was the last memory of her about her parents. After Alice's suicide, Emma spent a whole week staring at the shelf where she had kept the picture; she didn't speak to any of us, nor did she eat anything other than mere water. That was when my niece and others decided to leave the city for her to make a change. Even though it did make a change in her lifestyle, she still couldn't speak for a month and a half, now that she is willing to tell her stories to another person."

"Isn't that a good thing?" William asked

"Yes, indeed, but seeing how things are going now, it doesn't feel like she decided to share it with another person; she should also let it go, but it doesn't seem like that to me anymore. I am afraid she will get hurt even worse this time. I can't bear to do so, and I can see this was exactly because

Elle, I mean Elisa, had disagreed with her, even though I am not sure what is going on," She completed. William let out a sigh.

Then there was another moment of silence until William broke it, "How long do you known Emma's parents?" That question was out of the blue.

"Long enough that I would say almost my whole childhood was with them, like I was raised by them, why?"

"No, just asking," He replied.

"I can understand you concern as both her guardian and a person she had spent her childhood with, but I can assure you, this isn't going to hurt her, or at least if I think anything that we are going to do is dangerous, I will back off, as well as persuade her to do so, even though it is a bit complicated to explain what is really going on, or in other ways, you can say we are trying to find what is really going on, but the best you can do now to help her is to get her the information we require, I can understand it is a little unsatisfying answer if you were expecting me to persuade her to give up at the very first step, but you know her better, would she even if I told her to"

I knew their conversation was over, so I quickly went to the couch again and sat like someone who had not heard any of their conversation.

"Since you have come all the way to here, how can I turn you down, well about your therapist, I may have her number somewhere, but I can't assure you, it has been a long time, and about the police and the doctor, I remember the name of the doctor being Blake Wader, he worked at the hospital where you had been admitted, Good Life, but don't have any information about the police officer, I have forgotten his name, it was something like Carl or something, I don't really remember"

That was all I needed. I took my notepad and left the house with William. I got into the car. "Was your family picture that important?" He asked me to fasten the seatbelt.

"What?" I asked innocently as if I really didn't hear their conversation at all. "I know you eavesdropped, Hazel, you were really bad at hiding," He said.

Jesus, was I really that bad at hiding? "Did Aunt know too?" He nodded.

***

Aunt told me that she would message me the therapist's contact. "William, would you help me check the messages?" I told him while driving to my next location, which I was sure of, Good Life Hospital.

He switched on my phone as I heard tons of notifications "Um yeah I might as well as read every notification, 67 missed calls from 'Elder Sissy', 27 missed calls from 'Aiemee' and 7 missed calls from 'Mentally retarded teenager'" He read the notifications aloud, well I was sure I was not asking for these notifications, but 67 missed calls? I doubt if it has been 67 minutes since I left. I doubt if Elle would let me get inside the house again. "Really? Mentally retarded teenager?" He didn't even try to hide the laugh. "Does Lena know?"

103

"It was not long ago that she found out I saved her as 'troublemaker'; it has been 'mentally retarded teenager' ever since," I replied.

"None from Aunt?" I asked. "Yeah, the contacts are here," He said.

It was a long journey, but it hasn't been a long time since I last came; it was some days ago. Thank God I left early, even though it was for not notifying others, I managed to reach there at 10:30ish. I parked in front of the hospital. We walked towards the front desk. The blonde nurse at the front desk smiled at us. That smile almost felt similar to that of our school nurse back then; they somewhat looked similar too.

"We would like to know whether Dr. Blake Wader works here," William asked the nurse. "Just a sec," She looked into the computer screen in front of her.

"Oh, no, not anymore, Dr. Blake Wader retired a year ago," She replied. So that opportunity was blocked.

"Can we get his contact number if possible?" I asked. "I'm afraid we can't provide you with that," She said. "It would be so helpful if you could get any details about him. This is my contact number," I wrote down my number on a page of my notes and gave it to her. We walked out of the hospital.

William sighed as we got into the car. "Hey, don't back off, we still got two more." We drove towards a comparatively less crowded place. I took out my phone and saved the number Aunt had sent me. I dialed the number and put it on speaker. "Hello," A frail voice took the call. "Oh,

Hi, my name is Emma, I would like to know if you're Miss. Natalia Sarah," I said, even though I was sure that voice sounded younger than she could be. "I am her daughter, and I am sorry, she passed away last November," She replied. "Oh no, I am sorry for your loss, thank you for letting me know, wish you a good day." And like that, I hung up. The second person in the list was ruled out.

We sat in silence after hearing that Natalia had passed away. And I had no idea what I should do about the police officer; I don't even remember his name. "What should we do? About the police officer, we don't even know his name," I said, disappointedly.

"I do," He said. "What?" I asked, confused. "Silly, your parents' case was a major news back then, wasn't it? Is it that hard to know about the officer in charge when we have internet? You just need to look at the news reports back then!" And that was only when that idea popped up in my mind, too. I opened Chrome and searched '*Car accident 2006, 8* died' and there it was. I didn't even need to type all of their names; there were tons of news reports, some even saying it was a ghost and the highway was haunted.

And I got the name of the police officer, Carl Michael, but the longer I searched, another news report popped up, with Carl Michael, not about my parents, I read the headline loud *'Police officer died in Fire accident'* William snatched the phone from my hands, he read the rest of the news *'Our brave police officer Carl Michael died in the act of rescuing people from the building where a fire was let out on 19th November, though he saved the citizens, he had to sacrifice himself to death during this process, our city will-'* And like that, I saw his face going pale, like he had seen a ghost. He repeatedly searched other news reports, though they were the same as this one, searching if the date was correct.

"Are you okay?" I asked, though I didn't know what was going on. "Yeah, no, I need to take some fresh air," He got out of the car. I was still confused. What was in the news report that tensed him so much? I read the news report again and again. Still, I couldn't find anything more. I got out of the car, and the air was cold, even though it was quarter past eleven.

He was staring at his mobile phone, reading a text, maybe. "Hey!" I called him. He got scared that he dropped the phone, I tried to pick it up, but he nervously picked it up and said 'Thanks'. "You okay?" I asked, "You don't look quite okay. Do you have a fever? Why did you get disturbed while seeing the news?"

"Yeah, maybe I have a fever, I don't quite get up early, maybe because of the cold air in the morning." He didn't answer my other questions. "You want medicine, maybe a thermometer so that we can check the temperature," I said, opening the trunk and taking out a medicine box.

"You even carry a medicine box with you?" He asked. I smiled "Well I was quite of a 'sick kid' that nobody can expect when I will get sick, like when seeing similar highways or similar car that of my parents, I will feel like throwing up or will have a terrible fever, I know that sounds a bit absurd, but yeah, someone had even asked me why I was the only one who was over-exaggerating while my friends also had lost their parents but was a bit more normal than I was, I know it's strange" I replied.

He gave me that pitiful look, "Oh no, not that look, I grew up seeing people look at us in some kind of pathetic way when they hear that we're orphans," I said, giving him the thermometer.

"Well, actually, I don't think I need to check my temperature; it's not that bad." He handed me the thermometer back.

"But seriously, why did you panic over that date? I asked. "Well, it is more of a ridiculous reason," He said, turning his eyes from me to the dense forest behind us. "Well, I wouldn't mind unless it is ridiculous enough as a person who screwed up history class because of the fact that Germany invaded Poland on 1st September during WW2, which was the same date his 13th girlfriend dumped him," I said.

He burst out laughing, "Wait, actually, someone did that? Who would?" He said, controlling his laughter. "Sam, an old friend," I said, recalling Sam's ridiculous reasons for ruining a class. "I only regarded him as a friend because of the fact that he helped me cheat a couple of times, and I was silently grateful to him for interrupting every history class, because I hated them."

"I didn't think a straight-A student would cheat," He said mockingly. "Well, just because it was politics, and how did you know I was a straight A student?"

"A wild guess, maybe." It was a joke, but still, I could see him hesitating while I asked that. "Unless you got obsessed with me the time you met me at the library and were stalking me ever after," I said, laughing at my own joke. "Whoa, don't flatter yourself, young lady," He replied. "Like it is a thing to brag about," I said. "Well, it is a thing to brag about when it is a handsome young man like me," He said.

I suddenly took some steps back. "Oh my god, can I touch the ground, can I?" I asked. "What, what happened?" He asked nervously, "No, it's just the ground is full of the precious lies you have just dropped."

"Hazel! Seriously!"

That was when I got a call from the hospital. "Hello, is this Ms. Emma?" She asked. "Yes, this is," I replied. "We are so sorry to inform you that the Dr. Blake Wader you asked for passed away last November." I hung up the phone without saying anything. William was staring at me.

"Blake Wader's dead," I said. "Don't you think it is fishy that every other person who knew about my memory loss died? And in the same month," He seemed to be lost in thoughts.

CHAPTER 21

March 21, 4:33 pm

We reached our building, had some burgers on the way, but still I'm starving. I climbed up the stairs to the second floor. "Okay then," I said, continuing to climb the stairs until I heard Elle yelling from down below. I wonder if there are no neighbor complaints. "Yeah, I'm doomed," I said, looking behind to William, who was starting to walk away but stopped hearing her yelling. "By the way, if you are going to attend my funeral, please do not bring a wreath of red roses; white will do," I said. "Will white chrysanthemums do?" He asked back. "Yep, very well."

I walked towards our room. And just like that, there was a one-hour lecture before she let me in. "I'm not asking you where you went, I called Aunt, but Emma, I'm telling you, we don't have a place for another breakdown of yours!" She yelled, slamming her door really hard.

"How did it go?" I got a message from William. "If I don't do anything, that psycho will kill us; the police aren't going to do anything, but if I do something, Elisa is not going to let me off the hook," I replied. "So are you going to give up?" He texted back, "In either way I am to die, why give up?"

***

March 22, 8:33 am

Lena woke me up in the morning to go shopping. The main agenda is to buy Elle a nice outfit. It has been a while since she bought clothes for herself, and as she is a little heated up these days, it might help to soothe her. (Bribe!)

Little did I know Lena would backstab, well, not technically, it was her excuse for me and William to meet up. She invited him to go with us and escaped in the middle, saying the most ridiculous excuse ever, "Oh my god, I forgot to paint my nails, I don't usually go out without painting my nails, what about this, you guys go ahead, I'll take a taxi to go back home." That was what she said. At least she could have said she wasn't feeling well. I am going to deal with her when I go back.

We went to the mall in the middle of the city. If I had known picking a dress would be this troublesome, Lena video called me when we reached the shop. "I was trying to give you some alone time but I have no confidence in you picking a dress so I might trouble you a bit, I will hang up after we pick a dress for her, then you can do some shopping if you want to, if you know you know" and like that, I may have tried every single dress in that shop, but she wouldn't

110

just agree, when I picked a black sweatshirt, she said the color was inauspicious, when I picked a red floral dress, she said it was too girly for her, and like that she rejected every single dress. William, on the corner, was trying to control his laugh. At the end, I just hung up.

We then started to look for other outfits. A little time later, Will picked up five dresses and came to me. "All of these look okay. Maybe you can try it on to see if it really is."

The first one was a black oversized t-shirt with a print of a white butterfly

"Pass"

Then the second one, a pink jumpsuit

"Pass"

Then the same happened to the third one. The fourth one was a black knee-length off-the-shoulder dress with a floral design. He stared at me for a moment.

"This one will do," He said. But unfortunately, it was not a long-sleeve dress; Elle wouldn't wear that. "But Elle doesn't like this kind of dress," I said, looking at the mirror beside me.

We at last picked the fifth one, which was a white crop top with puff-style long sleeves. We went to the counter to pay. "Your total is 124". I looked at William. "No, you might have made a mistake. I looked at the tag before buying, it was not 124," I said. When that girl at the counter was going to say something, William came in front and paid for it. "Hey! But they made a mistake," I said, but he was dragging me out of the store. "They didn't, Hazel. I bought the black dress; it looked good on you, and you don't have to pay for it, I did."

I highly suspect that he had heard what Lena had said when she called. We walked towards the entrance until I noticed my necklace was not around my neck. I stopped. "My necklace," I said, and started nervously looking for it. I could tell the people who were passing by were giving me stares. William also looked confused. "Is that necklace important?" He asked, joining me in searching. "Hell yes!" I yelled. I started to go back to the way we walked just now, looking back and forth. I looked miserable until someone tapped my shoulder from behind. "Lost and Found!" William exclaimed that he had my necklace in his hands. "Since there's a rule that whoever found it gets to keep it, should I keep it?"

"Dare you!" I said, snatching my necklace from him. "You looked like a kid who lost her toy and was about to cry over it, kind of cute though." He smiled. "You want me to push you from this 4th floor?" I asked, though my eyes were tearing up. I could never imagine losing it.

We went back to the car. And there it is, a damn traffic jam. From the morning till now, I think things are going against me. I didn't even have breakfast. William got out of the car to see what was happening outside. He came back a few minutes later with a packet of bread. "Hey, how'd you know I was hungry?"

"Your stomach was loud enough, there's an accident ahead, it may take a while," He said.

“Maybe in the meantime we can talk about something,” He said.

“Like what?”

“Like life”

“Like, when did you get your license?”

“Like, why did you go crazy over a necklace?”

“It was my mother who gave it to me, it was the last thing she had given to me, it means a lot to me, a lot, every time I look at it, it feels like my mother never left, of course, that is never going to happen, whether I remember or not, it did happen in front of me didn’t it?” When I said that, I felt like I was lying to myself, like I didn’t want to believe it. After all these years, what all my therapists I’ve ever consulted failed to do was this too, make me believe and accept, it just never happened though.

“Do you remember anything about how you got there, like weren’t you with your friends before that, your Aunt also had told me it was her fault not noticing you enough that she didn’t notice you go missing” I really don’t know why he was asking all of this, is he just curious or why am I feeling like being interrogated.

I couldn’t hold back my tears. And this was exactly why no one has talked about this to me. But I felt a lot lighter. “I’m sorry if that made you uncomfortable, but you know what, after I lost my mother, I really thought that was the end, I lost all my belongings, everything that reminded me that my mom existed, I thought the world would forget her, you can say my most frightening nightmare was me myself forgetting her, that she would disappear from my memories as she did from my life, but it has been long enough for me to understand that you don't necessarily need a physical belonging to make them live among us, as long as they did once, they will continue to do so, as long as they live in our memories"

The traffic jam was over.

I reached our apartment holding two bags. "You should've told me before going, and I do have enough clothes," Elle said. "Don't worry, it's a full sleeve," I said, putting those down on the couch. "C'mon, Elle, it's been years, and you are still not moving on?" Amy asked. I don't know why she couldn't, but I think I can understand when she couldn't and what she feels when she couldn't.

CHAPTER 22

March 22, 6:37 am

I woke up hearing something fall from my desk. I turned the lights on to see what was going on. There it was, another letter, which I'm pretty sure others have also received.

Greetings, Emma Elizabeth Austin

I think you are too invested in me. I heard you did some digging? Well, wish you all the best on that. But I may warn you, to look out for your partners, like I said, take your time trusting others. In this envelope, there is another case that is yet to be solved. I swear it is much more interesting than the first one! You have two weeks.

Solve For X

Apart from this were some news reports. I opened the news report. *'Police officer died in fire outbreak...'* It was the same news report we saw when searching for Carl Michael. Attached to it was a... death certificate? I opened it, it was Carl Michael's. I changed my glare to the time of death, between 7 and 8 'o'clock in the evening of 19th November. Cause: Suffocation.

I got up from my bed and rushed to the living room; everyone had gathered there.

I grabbed Amy's envelope, though I expect the same letter in it. But it was not, the news report, it was not of a fire outbreak. *'Condolences: To our former colleague and an awesome friend, Blake Wader – Good Life Hospital.'* My hands trembled as I took the death certificate. Time of death: Between 5 and 6 o'clock in the evening of 22nd November. Cause: Head injury causing internal bleeding. I looked at Elle, with not fear but shock in my eyes, I knew, she knew, who was the next person, and why. She handed me hers, as I read the name, Natalia Sarah, *'Dead Body Found On Lake: Retired therapist Natalia Sarah was found dead on the lake near her house, her family member stated that she slipped and fell into the river while searching for her nephew, George....'*. Time of death was between 7 and 8 'o'clock in the evening of 26th November, cause: suffocation. I glanced at Elle again. This time, it was terror.

If I got Carl Michael, Elle got Natalia Sarah, and Amy Blake Wader, then what did Lena get? And William? I took Lena's envelope, and it was Blake Wader's, the same letter as Amy's.

A knock shook me from my thoughts. It was William; this time, he came over, and yes, he did receive a letter, but one thing special about all his letters was that the addressing part was torn away. I ran my eyes over his letter to see if he got Carl Michael's. I, William, and Carl Michael, Amy, and

Lena got Blake Wader, but there is only one person left, that is Elle, then who might be the other one, if this is supposed to be a two-member game?

I stared at William, who was the only person who knew how these people were connected, excluding Elle, who got a little glance at my notes. We explained it to others. "Seems like you two had already been a step ahead of us" said Lena. "Only if Elle hadn't disagreed, you all would have been there when we were investigating, but one thing that is sure now, we were on the right track," I replied.

My phone was buzzing in a corner, which I hadn't noticed until William did. It was not an unknown number. I hadn't saved it yet. It was Natalia Sarah's daughter, whom I had talked to the day before yesterday, but with a different number. I and William exchanged glances as soon as I heard her name. I picked up the phone and put it on speaker. "Hello?" a fragile voice, which I had heard. "Is this Miss Emma?" She asked. "Oh yes, it is, I had called you the day before yesterday," I replied.

"Yes, I remember, and that is why I called. May I know why you looked for my mother?" She asked. I paused for a moment or two. "Um, it is… nothing special really. She used to be my therapist years ago, and now I'm in a very good state (and that was a big lie), so I wanted to thank her." I managed to make up a reason that didn't sound absurd. "Oh, are you sure it was the only reason? I really wish you could tell me if there's more. I have been receiving various weird letters these days, and I-"

William took my phone. "Is it where a weird guy who likes to address himself as 'hunter' talks about some strange crap and how you are a part of an absurd game where you must solve cases?" And I agree that was a good way to explain what was happening these days.

"Yes," She said, and I knew who the other person with the Blake Wader death certificate was. I invited her to come to our house. Elle stared at me as I did.

"What are you doing, Emma Elizabeth Austin!?" Elle shouted at me. "Are you determined to go behind all these? Are you crazy, Emma? I didn't file a case because it was burdensome. But that doesn't mean it is your job, whoever this hunter is, I don't care; this could be another lunatic. At the end, the one who would be left behind is *you*. What happened the last time? Do I need to remind you of what happened? You didn't speak a word for a whole month! Do you think you're the only one who has lost everything? We did too, Emma, we did too!"

William tried to calm her down, but this was the first time after a long time that she had exploded like this. Lena pulled Elle. "You had short-term amnesia, we all cared for you, more than we cared for ourselves. We had lost our parents too, at the same time, Emma, we tried to pull ourselves together, not because we were bold, but because you were weak! You were always weak, and for you, we remained strong.

Have you ever thought of our mental state when you have yourself broken while trying to figure out things that don't even matter to you? Maybe because you don't care what happens to you afterwards, but have you ever thought of us, thought of Aunt? She had to change jobs again and again and again because of *you* –” William stopped her from saying anymore, but he shouldn’t have, *I* shouldn’t have.

I didn’t think that my actions would be a burden to them; in fact, it had always been. They just didn’t tell me. I was a burden when I had memory loss, because I couldn’t remember what happened, so they had to close our parents’ case because I couldn’t. I was being troublesome when I decided to investigate Alice’s case; in the end, she did suicide. Nothing I ever started will end up nicely. Everyone around me just disappears because of that, because of me. So did my parents, so did my teacher, and now, it is normal for her to think that the next would be them. I didn’t say a word, even when she went back into her room. I sat there, immobilized. My eyes filled up. But I managed not to cry, after all these years; that was the only skill I’ve mastered.

“She didn’t mean that–” I stopped Amy from consoling me. I stood up, walking to my room. William tried to stop me. “She had a point, Will,” I told him, managing not to make my voice sound like I’m going to cry the next second. I went to my room. Our house went unusually silent. I don’t know how, but I fell asleep somehow.

***

I woke up feeling a hand brushing my hair. I didn’t open my eyes, but I could say it was Elle. She let out a heavy sigh. “Em, you probably will not hear me, but–” she paused for a moment. “I just want you to know that I was wrong, and that I’m sorry. And I want to thank you, thank you for everything.

When our parents died, I felt like the world was ending, like it crashed in front of me. When I looked around, I couldn't see anyone but emptiness. The world felt … lonely. There was nothing that I could hold onto. I thought of why I was living if there was nothing in the world for me. But then I saw you, lying in a hospital bed, hopeless and clueless, with Lena and Amy. At that moment, I knew what I had in this world; I was older than any of you.

I knew I needed to protect you; it was not a burden but an escape, a reason for me to stay stronger. If not, then I didn't know why I should have, I would've probably lost my control. I–"

I got up from the bed and hugged her, tears running through my cheeks. She was crying too. We sat like that for a long time, long enough for me to notice that she was not wearing a long-sleeved top; her wound was visible. I lose my grip to look at her. "Why aren't you wearing a long-sleeve top? Your wound it's visible," I said.

"It is, Emma. I lived these years, thinking that covering up a scar would heal it, but it didn't. Just because you can't see it, doesn't mean it isn't here. It took me this much time to realize that covering up a scar would only make it worse. I'm sorry."

CHAPTER 23

March 22, 8:57 am

Freya Sarah Donald, Natalia's daughter, had come to our apartment. We're sitting around a table, like a secret group, trying to figure out what is really happening. Freya started the conversation, "On 26th November, we had a family gathering at our place. Around 7 in the evening, my mother went to the lake nearby to find my little cousin, George, but she didn't return even after George did. When we asked him, he said he had never seen my mother and that he came alone. Dad was concerned. So my uncle and dad went to the lake to find her. I think Uncle was the first one to find her, or her body.

She somehow fell into the lake, where we assumed maybe she had slipped, but I started to doubt that assumption after receiving the letters. A week after my mother died, anonymous letters came into my mailbox, at least one in a while, repeatedly, which I had burned some. All it contained was merely a few sentences like 'Your mother slipped and drowned, right? Or did she' or sometimes 'Do you want to know more?' and the recent ones saying 'I am starting to recognize you as a player and not a pawn, this game of chess doesn't have a king, your mission is not to protect the king but to find him' and something like 'Solve For X'" She stopped.

"I knew it, he is a freak who sees himself as a king and the center of the world or something," Lena yelled, crumbling the letters she got from the hunter; maybe she had imagined doing the same to him. Well, I had dreamed of choking him to death, as long as it is legal to do so in dreams, I will continue to do so. "Shh, Lena! He might be hearing us, or maybe he has some kind of tracker or something like that in this house or in your car, or maybe he is watching us from the apartment next door, anything is possible when he was able to know that we investigated those three," William whispered.

"Wait, I do think so too, maybe he has some kind of device here or at my home, if he knew about you two investigating, and he knew about me trying to call the police, he definitely has any" Freya said, and we agreed. The next few minutes, no hours, were spent on searching, searching for an unknown device we don't even know what it looks like. And disappointment. We checked thoroughly, through every wall and corner, but there were none. We sat down at the same places.

"Well, that was a dead end," Amy said, exhaustedly. "I think we have to rather analyze what is going on than to randomly search your house," William said, taking out my little note from his pocket, "Like Hazel did, yesterday, and it turned out that we were on the right track."

"Wait, how did you –"

"You left it in the car."

We started to write down our assumptions and facts, well, most of it was assumptions on a whiteboard that we had bought for no reason, maybe for studying and taking last-minute notes. Who are connected and how they are connected, and the first clues were Natalia Sarah, Blake Wader, and Carl Michael, which at last pointed to one person, Emma Elizabeth Austin, me. How I connected them was by using my memory loss. My memory loss was put as the center of the maze, and three lines connected it to Natalia Sarah, Blake Wader, and Carl Michael. Freya took the marker and drew another line that connected Natalia, Sarah, and Freya.

She turned to us. "I think I am the only one in this group who is directly related to these three, so let's start from me, and my mother," She said. Even though she had participated in this much, every time she mentions her mother, I could see pain, of losing her, and fear, of the fact that she could be murdered.

And the moment William heard this, he started questioning her. I wonder if he's a spy undercover. "Your cousin was there, right? What exactly did he say?" William asked her.

"Yes he was, but he is only seven, I don't know if we can take his words as true, after sometimes he said that he did see mom and that a shadow monster took mom away, I don't know, I was so frustrated at that time, that I couldn't accept the fact that mom was gone, so one day I burst out of anger and scared him, he has never talked to me again, I tried to apologize but it was of no good" What Freya had said clicked something on my mind 'Shadow monster'.

"Wait, Freya, what if it is just an if, but what your brother said was true? What if he really saw a shadow monster? Or a person who looked like a shadow monster to a seven-year-old," I said.

"But how can we know, it can be either; maybe the boy imagined all this, or the boy did see a man, we can't verify the facts," Elle said. And that was true. "We need more, but if we want to find this hunter, we have to play by his rules. We need to find him, and that is exactly the point of this game too, find the king, find him." William said, erasing my memory loss in the center to a corner and wrote 'hunter-the king?' there and continued,

"And the rules which I have assumed are that each two of us have three different persons to solve. I and Emma have Carl Michael, Freya and Elisa have Natalia Sarah and Amy and Lena have Blake Wader, so what to be done is that we have to investigate all of them, not just one, and maybe doing it separately might be effective, because I think it would be more easy if we go see their families, or the ones who were present during what happened to them, and gain more data, instead of just sitting here with our speculations"

And the terror turned into determination as I imagined once more of choking that freak.

CHAPTER 24

We went to the police station where Carl Michael worked. It sure took hours to come back to this city. I walked into the entrance, and a building in front of me that I could never forget, I have been here more than a couple of times, for a reason that I don't remember. I let out a heavy sigh. never thought I would come back here again, it was a nightmare, a really scary one.

"Ready for the investigation?" William asked. "Like our first destination is not a police station!" I murmured.

We stopped the first officer we saw, and as always, I was not good at making excuses, so William took charge. I took out the recorder from my handbag and turned it on.

"Hello officer, we're sorry to interrupt your duty, but could you spare a couple of minutes of yours?" He asked, in the calmest way possible, while I was crossing my fingers, I haven't felt this nervous while trespassing in a sealed territory or trying to find out who a serial killer is.

"Um, so we are doing a project about Carl Michael, the late police officer who worked here, so it would be helpful if you could say a few words about him." I don't think that would've worked with a normal police officer, but this one was a bit of a blabbermouth.

"Oh- I didn't know kids were actually doing projects about him"

"But here we are!" I said with a really awkward laugh.

"Carl was an officer who would always adhere to his principles, not to mention his work ethic. He was so devoted to being a police officer that it led to his divorce," He said.

"His divorce?" I asked, that was news to me, because when handling my case, he was happily married with a daughter of my age.

"Yeah, well, I've only heard of it, but ten years ago, there was a major car accident where eight people died. Carl was the officer in charge; the old officers who used to work with him say that Carl was obsessed with that case. Even when the case was closed, he believed something was wrong about this. He applied to reopen this case several times, but I'm not sure what the reason was. Every time it was declined, but I'm sure that case was not an ordinary case because it was highly confidential. Carl, when going after this case, didn't go home for several days. His wife and daughter were alone at home; his wife couldn't stand it, and divorced him not long after." That got me, I realized our family was not the only one that got shattered after our parents died. The reason why it was declined was also me, as long as I don't recall my memory, reopening won't happen.

"Do you think he was acting strange before he died?" That question came out of the blue. Thank God that police officer didn't think that much; if he had, we would have had to blow our covers.

"How did you know? Well, he was, he really was, Carl was a rather calm and alert person, but a couple of days before he died, he seemed rather… distracted. He couldn't focus on anything. There was one time when he was making instant coffee, but he didn't even notice the hot water overflowing. Thankfully, I noticed him in time, or he wouldn't have noticed even if he had burned his hand." We looked at each other. What could have gotten into Carl that much that he even forgot to feel pain?

"And oh yeah, I'm not sure if I am supposed to say this, but Carl was looking for a case file of something that happened a decade ago, the day he died, and he did find it and took it home." I don't know if this could be a clue, but if he was that much distracted, yet he searched for a case file that happened a decade ago, that must be important, right? Or could it be my parents' case? It also happened a decade ago. I turned to the officer again, but Will stopped me.

"And that's all for today, thank you, officer," He concluded and grabbed me. "Let's go," He whispered to me and turned to that officer. "And if possible, this is our email. Can you email which case file it was? Thank you again," He said and walked fast. "What happened?" I asked when we reached the exit.

"Didn't you see, many other officers were coming, it was our luck that we got a blabbermouth that he spilled all the tea, but if anyone else notices us, we're doomed," He said.

"Well, we did get enough tea, what about paying a little visit to Carl Michael's house?" Will asked, as if breaking into a late police officer's house sounded exciting.

"Not today, we need to go back right now. We decided to meet up at 8 at my apartment. We'll be late if we don't go now," I said.

CHAPTER 25

March 22, 8:38 pm

We reached our apartment by half past eight. We were the last ones to arrive. Elle and Freya seem to be friends by now; they are discussing something seriously. Amy turned to us, hearing the creaking sound of the door opening. Lena is furiously scribbling notes and crumpling them right away. We took our places at the meeting table, and the conference began. Amy and Lena stood up from their seats and came in front.

Lena signed Amy to start next. She stood up with a bunch of photos. I looked at each of them as she pinned it to the board. A house, an old one, Good Life hospital, and an old couple.

"So, these two are Blake Wader's parents; his father died not long ago, and the only relative he has left is his mother. She is currently in a nursing home. Last November 22nd, Blake Wader died because of a head injury. It is said that he slipped and fell, and his head got hit on a sharp edge of furniture. No one knows what happened as he lived alone. But I am starting to doubt it because of what is recently happening, this is not an accident, which I am very much certain of." Amy stopped and looked at Lena, hinting for her to continue.

"So, we went to his house, first of all, we didn't know at that time that he lived alone, we were just planning on visiting his mother, but as there was no one else, and we could say that the man barely had neighbors, and a window was left open…" Oh, and I knew what Lena was going to say; it's always been like this, recklessness at peak. But this time, it was what we needed, a bit of recklessness.

Lena continued, "So we entered the house, and it has been left as it was; no one came to clean it. And Oh Jesus, for God's sake, if they had cleaned the blood stain, but no, I know I can't just describe the place, so we recorded it," She said and took out her phone, swiping through it as she found the recording and played it, placing it on top of the table.

It started when they began to enter the house using that small window. Amy had to pull Lena to get in. A stuffy place, well, it's been months since a person lived here. There was a narrow path that led to the living room, and a calendar was placed on the wall of the path. They walked, silently, as if it were a haunted house; it looked like one. Spider webs on both sides, I could hear Amy making noises every time she saw an insect. The living room was the messiest one, a typical haunted one.

The camera focused on the blood stains at the edge of the table in front of the couch. Then it slightly moved, showing a laptop in the room right next to the living room, it was on a table, in front of a chair. The camera zoomed into the edges of the chair; there were several cut marks. Lena paused the video. "This is the first clue we've got, don't know if really a clue, but the cut marks show something was tied here, what could it be? A person for sure!" Lena exclaimed. "Not necessarily, nothing proves," Freya said, zooming the video again. "But the laptop –"

Right when I was going to ask about the laptop, Lena stopped me. "I know what you are going to say, so my intelligent brain had planned it ahead, I got the laptop!" She said, taking the laptop out of her bag. Oh goodness, she did not.

"Lena! That's private property!" I exclaimed, I really don't know what to say. "Like a house wasn't!" She replied.

"And you agreed?" Elle turned to Amy. "For context: I *did not* notice her taking that." Amy washed her hands.

"Well, she got it, it's done, no more yelling or blaming, let's see if we can open it," William said, and we all turned to Amy.

"Fine!" She said, taking the laptop in her hands. Out of everyone we know, Amy is the only, and probably the best, who can hack into systems; her computer skills are top-notch.

"But.. It may take a while, maybe tomorrow"

"Tomorrow?" I asked, I didn't think it would take that much.

"Yep, and I have to sleep too, if I skip that, maybe it will only take hours," Amy said, and we aren't in a rush.

Then it was Elle's turn to say what she had found. She stood up. "So, our first destination was the lake, we recorded a video of the place," She said, taking out her mobile phone and playing the video. A lake, vast and calm as if a body was never found here, in a peaceful place, but the peaceful it is, the stronger the storm is, the sky was clear as if it was the reflection of the lake itself, clear but frightening. The camera turned around, showing the dense forest behind it. Will anyone know a lake exists here if they watch from the outside of the dense woods? But why would they allow a seven-year-old to come to this secluded place?

While walking towards the lake, Freya stepped on something. She picked it up, and the camera focused on the thing, which was a necklace. I heard Elle asking Freya, "Is this your mother's?"

"No, it isn't," I heard Freya saying, and that's where the video ends. Freya took out the necklace from her jacket pocket and laid it on the table.

"Could this be hunters?" I asked, and everyone had the same opinion. "The lake is secluded, so no one really goes there, except for our family, and that day, there were only my mother, me, and my Aunt who uses necklaces, and this is of neither of us," Freya said. It is the hunter's and I'm sure about this.

"Did you check your mother's room?" Amy asked Freya. "No, we didn't, we tended to, but my Aunt is cleaning there today, so we can't, I can't risk alerting her of any situation, she is already heartbroken about my mother as much as I am, even though it's been months," She replied.

Now it was our turn to turn up our findings. William got up and started to talk. "We went to the police station Carl used to work in; we didn't think going to his ex would be useful; she hasn't contacted him since the divorce, and we asked one of the officers there about Carl." As he said this, he turned on the recording.

Everyone looked at me as the recording ended. "Did you go to his house?" Elle asked.

"No, we are planning to do so tomorrow," I said. We ended the conference and started to look for more clues from what we had gotten.

William called me out to the balcony. It was a half-moon day, like it was on the day Alice died. "What happened?" I asked. "I–I can't make it tomorrow," He said, and I noticed he had been trying really hard not to make any eye contact, and there was guilt in his eyes. "Why?" I asked. "It's my mother's birthday, I need to go see her at the graveyard," He said, but this time it was pain that I saw. "What was her name?" I asked, obviously, I was not good at comforting, but why did I ask that? There were many other options, Emma!

"Elora, um Elora …Cooper, yes Elora Cooper," He said. "Why are you stuttering? It's not like you're lying," I said with a laugh. "Do you hate liars?" He asked, and his voice was firm, like it was serious. "What happened? Well, why should anyone like liars?" I said back, Did I say the wrong thing? No right? Then why does it feel wrong?

"Yes, you're right, why should anyone like liars? No one likes liars." His voice was getting anxious, a bit disappointed.

"I – I've got a confession to make"

"Well…what is it?" I asked eagerly. "Well I- I-I, you know what, never mind"

"What! No, say it!" A voice asked even before I could. "Lena! Were you eavesdropping?" I yelled before I saw Elle, Amy, and Freya behind her. "You too, Elle?"

"Well, I …I just passed by, ya just passed by," saying this, they all returned to the living room. "Would you like to continue?" I asked.

"Let's go back to the living room," He said.

CHAPTER 26

March 23, 10:33 am

I am now in front of Carl Michael's house. This place is secluded. How did he live here? Elle and Freya had gone to the Welfare orphanage. Apparently, Natalia had visited that orphanage two days before she died; she had worked there years ago as a therapist. Amy and Lena are at home. Amy is trying to open the laptop, and Lena is accompanying her.

I walked towards the door. Sure, it was locked, but I had a solution; I cracked open one of the windows. Oh God, is this how thieves enter houses? How do they even make it? Well, I did, barely. I really hope I will not alert the police station. I got into the house, it had remained untouched since he died. His wife did not come to pack his things up or to clean the house. I took my phone out to record and started to search the house, each and every corner, under couches, on top of tables, under the bed, and everywhere. It was like the file he took disappeared into thin air. I leaned on the burning place, exhausted, until I noticed the paper remains in it. I kneeled down to see what it was; it could be a bunch of papers or the case file. I zoomed in so that it could be clearer.

Suddenly, I got an email and a call. I paused the recording.

"Hello?" I said.

"Oh, hello, it's, ah, you don't know my name, the police officer you talked to yesterday, my name is Lucas, I've emailed the case file Carl took, you owe me one for this kid," He said.

"Oh yeah, thank you, Lucas. Can you do me another favor? Were there any keys when they found Carl's body?" I asked him because no matter how hard I searched, there were no keys in the house, and it was locked.

"What an odd thing to ask, but yet, no, there were none, now you owe me two," He said.

"Thank you again," I said and hung up the phone. I swiped to the email, opening the case file. I read the name on it. The names on the file were Elora Dormen and Noel Dormen. Their last name is Elle's Aunt and uncle! And the strangest fact, their son survived, Daniel Dormen. It can be a crazy coincidence, right? That William's Mother's name is Elora? Two can have the same name, right?

I got a call, again, from Elle, my hands were trembling, and it took me a few seconds to answer the phone. "Hello, Elle?" I said, hoping it would be to ask me where I am or I have eaten. "Emma," she called me. She only calls me Emma in serious situations. "We found that Natalia asked for a kid's details, and it is of Daniel Dormen's." Her voice is getting sharper. "And… and on the visitors list, there is my name on the visitors list and my father's name" That crashed me, some crazy assumptions came to my mind, the letters, saying that the descendants of Dormen have weakened into *two*, William being a part of this whole thing, we doesn't even know why, the letters, they constantly repeated to not trust easily... Elle started to panic. "Em, I don't know, I don't remember having a cousin, I don't –"

"Elisa, Elle, no, don't panic, why should you? We can figure it out at home. Come home now, okay?" I said, even though my throat was getting dry. I got another call even before I hung up with Elle. It was Amy.

"Emma, I don't know what this means, but Blake Wader has last been to Good Life hospital's site, to look for a patient's details, and the patient was… Daniel Dormen:" No, why is everything pointing to Daniel Dormen? How is he even alive? I slowly leaned to sit down on the floor, my hands went to William's name on the contact, I pressed it, even though I didn't know what to ask, I just wanted to confirm, confirm that I was wrong. He picked up at the first ring. "Hey, got any clues, Hazel?" He asked, and I ran out of words to fill in the silence. "Hazel?"

"Will," I said, trying to figure out what next, "Do you… Can I ask you something?" I managed to speak. "What happened? Did you find anything?"

"William, what was your father's name?" That was a strange question to ask. "Yes…I do, what- what happened?"

"What is his name?"

"Noel," That was the last string I had held onto, and that was cut off, "Did you, by chance, live in Welfare orphanage?" There was no need to ask, but I did.

"How did you- Emma, what exactly did you find?"

"No, nothing, I just got emotional, I thought of my father, just out of the blue, but William, can you…Can you come home by 3?" I asked.

"Yes, yes, I can, you seem serious," He said. I wanted to cry out loud, but why did I? I've got no reason to, no, I can't cry, but my eyes didn't listen to its owner.

I hate liars, and I do.

CHAPTER 27

March 23, 3:15 pm

I entered my apartment, and everyone else was there, except William, or should I call him Daniel?

"Emma, do you think this Daniel is connected to Hunter, Elle said she doesn't remember having a cousin," Amy asked, and I bet they don't know about William.

"Maybe he *is* the hunter, you won't know who's lying and who's not." I leaned towards Elle and hugged her tight, tears running down my cheeks. "Emma, what happened?" She asked me, hugging me comfortingly.

Before I could answer, Daniel came in through the door. He turned to me, crying in Elle's arms. "What happened?" He asked, his voice softer as ever.

I pulled myself together and walked towards him. "William?"

"Yes," He answered.

"William," I called again.

"Yes. I'm here."

"William!"

"What happened, Hazel? Why are you calling me like that?"

"What? Can't I call you that? Isn't it your name?" I asked, my tears running down without my consent. A strange pain locked my mouth, I couldn't say more, but I did, I yelled.

"Tell me! Is it?!" I yelled as hard as I could, screamed until my throat went dry. Elle held me tight when she thought I was going to fall.

"Emma, I can, I can explain," He said, the most heard excuse, the most common one.

"Then explain, I ain't got time for liars, so explain your excuses and get lost! And I'll say for once and for all, I *hate* liars, and I do," I screamed, my steps were unbalanced.

"I tried to tell you yesterday, but –"

"So the 'confession' you meant was this?" Lena cut him off in the middle.

"Yes, but I wasn't brave enough –".

"*Poor Word Choice*," Lena said, grabbing me.

"What were you not brave enough for? To admit that you've been lying? To admit that your real name is not

William but Daniel? Or were you afraid to admit that you are a hunter? Or were you not brave enough to kill us, huh?"

"Hazel, I –"

"And, I have a name, and it's not Hazel or brown, it's Emma Elizabeth Austin, got it?"

"Have you said enough? If not, then we've had enough. Don't ever let your stupid face be in front of me again," Lena said.

He looked… disappointed, or sad? Or was it guilt? Why should he be disappointed or sad? Because he couldn't fool us again?

"Get out, right now!" Elle shouted at him.

"I'm sorry," He murmured before getting out.

CHAPTER 28

March 23, 6:34 pm

A knock on my door woke me up from sleep. I had been lying in bed all day after Will- Oh yeah, I didn't even know his name, after *Daniel* left. And somehow, I fell asleep; maybe I was too tired from all that screaming.

Lena opened the door. She had a bowl of fruit with her. "Oh, c'mon, don't tell me you think that I am sick," I said, getting up from the bed.

"We do think, and it's not just we think, your temperature is up, it's like 100°F. I got the medicine too," She said, carefully placing them on my table.

"Yeah, I got it, you can leave," I said, leaning back on my bed.

"Not until I see you take the medicine," She said, and I took the medicine.

From a distance, I heard a doorbell. Someone opened the door. "I told you to get lost!" I heard Elle yelling, and I knew it was Daniel. It does feel weird calling him Daniel.

I got up from the bed, Lena tried to stop me, but I didn't. I walked towards the door. "Let him in, Elle," I said. Only then did I notice that my voice had changed due to a cold. Elle looked at me, confused, and then opened the door.

"I I-I know that you must be mad at me, and I'm not here to change that, I deserve to be, but I think I owe you an explanation," He said. In his hands were tons of paper pieces. He handed them.

It was the torn addressing part in each of his letters; he was the one who tore it, because all of it had the addressing as 'Greetings Daniel Dormen', and then there were two letters, one from March 20 and another from 29th November. I opened the first one, that day he had lied that he didn't get any letters, he indeed did.

Greetings Daniel Dormen,

Nice approach to changing your identity, guess how I knew it? But what would you think they would do if they found out? Remember? Their parents killed your family! Don't try to find out how I know, but you're on your own

"Our parents did what?" I said out loud, there was no way they- I mean, don't he know *Elle* is his family? I quickly opened the other.

This was not making sense. If it was Carl who wrote this, he is supposed to be dead at that date, and clearly, his cousin is not dead.

"I initially approached you to avenge my parents, my uncle, Aunt, and of course my cousin Ellie, even though I lied about my identity, I never lied about them, I thought you didn't deserve the life you are living now, I thought it wasn't fair for you to live normally when I –, so I did it deliberately but, after we went for investigating together, I realized your life was… miserable than mine, I realized no matter what your parents had done, you didn't deserve to be punished for their actions, until we found when Carl Michel died, I was stunned, I really thought I was in the right, until I saw the date, not until then did I ever doubted that your parents didn't do it, but after that, I did, after all this time, I was the one who was in the wrong, I –"

"Of course, our parents didn't do it, because they were your uncle and Aunt, you stupid!" Elle shouted, and I could see he was confused, *not acting,* really confused.

"What?" He asked.

"Do you know Elle's full name?" Amy asked, and surely he didn't.

"Elisa William Dormen," Lena said, and oh god, why was it funny to see his reaction? I'm not supposed to laugh, I'm not supposed to laugh, and oh yeah, I did.

"Wait – so, no, this isn't working out, what is going on?" He asked.

"Your uncle William and Aunt Emily had died along with our parents, but not your cousin, Ellie was Elisa's pet name when she was a kid, and the whole time, you was taking revenge for your cousin on your cousin" Amy said, "And oh yeah, that letter from Carl Michael is also wrong, our parents would never do that."

This whole crap is messed up, and that is the only thing I know.

"You could have told us! If you doubted it after we found out about Carl, then why didn't you tell us?" I asked, but my question was interrupted by Lena.

"Wait, so you are Elle's cousin brother?" Elle and William nodded.

***

Daniel and I went to the balcony. "Well, should I call you Daniel or William? It's kinda weird thinking of you as

Daniel…and let's be real, the name William is far better than Daniel."

"You're aware that you are talking about *my name*, right?" He asked. I didn't say anything until he took a photo from his pocket, a photo that I'm very familiar with, my family picture, the one that got stolen.

"Sorry, I was the one who took it," He said.

"So the bucket guy was you!" I shouted.

"Wait, you all figured out it was me? Like I thought I was fully undercover with that painting bucket guy look."

"Oh well, let's say your plan was not quite impressive, a never-seen-in-entire-life guy bumping into you, and boom, your house key gets stolen! Does that make you less suspicious? And, don't let Elle know it was you, or else she would blow the house for that, you almost ruined her clothes," I said.

"You asked me why I didn't tell you all, it's because it was too late, too late to confess that if I did, maybe I'll never see you again, and at the end of the day, impersonating is a crime" He said, not looking at me, his eyes were fixed on the moon, and I could say he regretted it, and great, now I regret yelling at him.

He finally turned to me, "I have something to tell you, this time, it's serious," He said. I may need all the possible definitions of serious. I was about to say something, right when I heard something fall.

"Oh Holy–my phone!" Lena came out from her hiding spot. "Oh no," She said, how could someone make that awkward smiling face when they have been caught for eavesdropping twice.

"I was just passing by, but it would be an honor if I could also hear the important-serious-thing?" She shamelessly continued to stay here, and Daniel didn't object. I can say a death sentence or life imprisonment is worth killing that thing.

"Um, the serious thing?" I asked him, and he took out his phone and took messages.

"This is also the reason why I didn't tell you the truth, on that day, when we went to your city to find out about those three, I meant to tell you the moment I saw the date when Carl Michael died, but suddenly, I got a message," He said, and showed us the message.

Dan, do you think she will accept the fact that you were lying to her the whole time? You need to know something about Em, that she never, ever, liked liars.

Dan? So the messenger knew his true identity, and the way they talked about me, about me not liking liars, it's like they know me better. "Is it the hunter?" I asked, though I thought it wasn't.

"No, it can't be, girl, have you ever seen him addressing us like that? And you 'Em'. Nah, there's no way that he would address you to anything that isn't Jr. Austin or Miss Emma Elizabeth Austin," Lena said. And she was right, but then who could it be?

"At that moment, I knew I screwed up and there was no going back, because if I did, you all would hate me for

147

lying, and I thought there was no harm in changing my name, like I don't have any other intentions, other than finding this whoever-the-hunter is" Daniel said, but my mind was still on the message phrase. I and Lena figured it out at the same time.

"The number!" We said loudly at the same time, and Daniel looked confused. "We know the number, this number messaged us also, the day we found Alice, it was the messenger who told us to go to Western Seashore, and that is how Em found Alice," Lena said.

"Yes, but it's no use in finding that, we did try to locate who this messenger was, but we couldn't, not even the police could." Lena sighed.

"Well, I think it's a signal for us to go back to the investigation!"

CHAPTER 29

March 23, 8:43 pm

Freya had said she would be staying tonight, so would Daniel, so that we would have more time to look after the clues we have now (Another table conference), since I broke out when we were supposed to have one.

Freya stared at her mother's death certificate. "Do you think finding something will do any good? My mother, she, everyone thinks that she slipped, but don't you think it is a less painful explanation than murder?" She said in a low voice.

"You know what's scarier? Living, knowing that a person is out there, who murdered your own mother, and most likely will do the same to you, and breathing, when you know there is a possibility you won't be able to do that the next moment" Lena said, this time, she was serious, *serious* that I could see the fear she explained right in her eye.

"But that's not painful as it is when you are living, knowing that the person you love the most isn't here anymore, and breathing, when you know that person can't do it anymore" Daniel said back, and the room went silent, and I could bet that everyone had a figure in their mind now, of the person they lost, the one they never thought they would, and it was a not-so-coincidence that we all had someone we lost.

"And that is why we need to find it because we lost the person we love the most, and there is a man out there who might be the reason for it," I said.

Freya's eyes were still fixed on the death certificate and the pictures, but this time, her eyes were locked on something else. "Hey," She said in a low voice, "This mark, it wasn't there, my mom never had it," she said.

We took the photos of her; there was a mark on the left ankle of Natalia, a mark around her ankle, like she had worn an anklet for a long time, or like someone had had a tight grip around it that left a mark.

Daniel took the photo and pinned it among the others on the board, and stared at it. "Do… we have evidence that they were murdered?" He muttered.

"What?" Amy asked. "Rather than the letters, do we have any evidence that they were murdered? We always looked for the murderer, whom we assumed was the 'hunter,' but we skipped the first step. If we were a detective, why would we think they were murdered?"

Yes, we didn't, we didn't think of how they might have died, never about how we thought they were murdered,

Natalia could have slipped, Carl's could be an accident, so could've been Blake's, he's old, living alone, and accidents can happen. But the mark changed Natalia's one; her own daughter swears she had never seen that mark on her mother, maybe not even the minutes before she was gone, and that mark can't possibly exist without any external force, which could be intentional.

"Does your mom wear any ornaments like anklets?" Lena asked. She was probably thinking the same as I.

"No, never any ornaments, not even an earring or a necklace, she was strict in those, never forced me to not wear them, but would always say something about having self-discipline and control over yourself and blah blah blah's which I never really paid attention to, but I can certainly say, she didn't wear those, any around her ankle, no, no, never.." Those no's and never were something she said to herself, and was muttering it again and again.

But that was familiar, the fear, or the pain, the misbelieve, though she's sure of what she doesn't want to make sure, I've done that too, many times, many times that some saw me talking to the blank walls where I presumed my parents were standing, but all they could see was a crazy orphan talking to the walls.

"Hey… don't…" Elle was trying to comfort her but she didn't know how to.

I stood up and walked towards her, but no, wait, I stopped at the view of Lena's laptop screen. It was playing the video of them entering the house, and the calendar hung on the path that led to the living room…

"Did you check the calendar?" I asked suddenly "The month, it's May" And that is when they noticed it too, the month on the calendar is May, not November, but Blake Wader died on November, no one been there since then, other than us, then why is May, or it could be he was lazy to change it from May onwards?.. Or maybe not

"On it, Em, we are going to check it now." Amy and Lena got up and went to Blake Wader's house.

***

The room went silent again, and everyone returned to searching for other clues. We confirmed that the paper pieces found in the fireplace were the case file. Amy found the remains of unburned paper in the fireplace, and some of them were clearly remains of the case file.

I'm watching the news reports of the fire accident, the accident in which Carl Michael died, fire fighters running in, people running out, the siren of ambulances, reporter's were there by then, like the news spread quickly than it should, of course, causing trouble to the rescue officers, the camera went in the building, the fire was extinguished by now, most of the people were out, and yeah, not Carl, the reporters rushed in, I mean for what? The rescue officer was kicking the door open, several of them, one was running with a child in his arms, and one was kicking the door open. The camera went inside, a burned face… one I recognize, Carl Michael's, but wait, the officer kicked the door open? I played that part again and again. Yes, the officer did kick the door open, so the door was locked? Then how did Carl get in? Or …

"Daniel!" I yelled. Daniel was checking the other death certificates. "C'mon, look at this," I said. Freya and Elle came to look at it too.

"What happened? What's wrong with it?" Elle asked.

"The door, it looks like it was locked, the officer had a hard time opening it, but Carl did enter the room, and the video doesn't show any other exits, so that means someone had locked the door after Carl entered, which means that the fire was not an accident," Daniel said as if reading my mind.

"And that the killer was there when the accident happened, maybe as one of the rescued people," I said, and continued to repeat the video again and again, the part where people rushed out, but there were many, many that it was impossible for me to recognize any of them as the hunter. Daniel and Elle started to watch it too, for quite a long time, long enough that I was into it and didn't notice the phone buzzing.

"Your phone," Freya pointed out. It was Lena's video call, I answered.

"You were right, detective, there is something behind the calendar." Lena switched the camera, and the wall of Blake's house came into view, the wall behind the calendar, and there were… blood stains? Or was it paint?

"They are blood stains, Em, don't have to stare no more, I checked it," Amy said from the other side.

Blood stains on the wall, and a calendar to cover it, was it left by the hunter? Was it him who covered the stain? So–

A voice cut my thoughts off; it was from the phone. "Hey! What are you two doing there?" A male voice, did they get caught?

"Um, we… we are from the, uh… the cleaning company, yeah, right, the cleaning company!" Lena said, and the camera was no longer focused on the blood stain. Lena might have put it in her pocket, but didn't hang up.

"Cleaning company?" the voice repeated back

"Yeah, Mr. Blake's family wants us to clean up the house, you know, even the blood stains are still here, so"

"No you're not, you two are not from the cleaning company, Mr. Blake doesn't have any relatives other than the distant ones, who may or may not have even known that Mr. Blake died, the only close relative is his mother who is currently at the nursing centre, so tell me, was it one of you who also came last November 22nd?"

Last November 22nd? Like the November when he died?

Amy asked the same question. "Weren't it- wait, there's something wrong here, you're coming with me, to the police station," He said. And I heard some noises, and some chaos, they hung up the call.

I tried to call them again, but Freya cut me off.

"I found something."

CHAPTER 30

March 23, 11:12 pm

The door opened. it was Amy and Lena, they're back. And we were waiting for them to get back, waiting for Amy to get back, precisely, we needed her.

"That boy! Oh my–We would have ended up in the police station if not for us running away!" Lena said, drinking a cup of water–From *my* cup.

Well, I didn't have time to argue with her; there was something more important, more important than my cup.

"Remember the day we went to investigate alone? After Elle restricted me? That day, the number we used to call Freya was not the one she has now, fair enough, her mother died and she now uses her mother's phone, but the number my Aunt used to contact, the number we used first to contact Freya, was the second phone Natalia had, the phone she used to contact patients, she had a separate one for it, and today, Freya happened to check that phone, and look what she found"

I passed the phone to them, the phone was filled with threatening messages from a number which she saved as H. He threatened her to get the files of my treatment, and she did give it to him, for her daughter's life, on 18th November. She gave it to him at the lakeside.

The next day, on 19th November, when she was having the family get together, this H, who is probably the hunter, messaged her to come to lake shore, she might have thought he had her nephew in control, so she freaked out and went to the woods to search for him, but, her nephew hadn't mentioned anything about it, which means it was probably his trick. And the mark on her leg happened when he pulled her into the water.

So, he knew about my memory loss from her. Freya was even more scared now, and broken, but then there was revenge in her eyes, and I could tell now she would do anything to find that hunter.

Now, everything was a bit clear, according to the dates, he went to Carl Michael first, and then may have threatened him also, for Elora and Noel's case file, then Carl Michael takes the case file to his home, he might not be the one who burned the case file, because this hunter learned about Daniel from the case file. So after bringing it home, he gets the alert of the fire, and goes to the fire site, where this hunter was hiding, to kill him. He locks Carl in the room, then escapes. He might be the one who took the case file, because no one else had the key to his house, and it was not found in either the house or in his body, so probably, Hunter might have taken it, then got the file and burned it afterwards.

As per the case file, he finds out that Daniel was admitted to Good Life Hospital, and the doctor who consulted him was Blake Wader. As the person who saw Amy and Lena said, he might have gone to Blake Wader's house on 22nd November, and then captured him. The blood stains on the wall might be from when he captured Blake Wader. Then he threatens him to get the info about Daniel, and then finds that Daniel stayed at the Welfare Orphanage. He then kills Blake Wader and then escapes through the window, as the people said the door was closed when they found the body.

And thirdly, he went to the Welfare orphanage and got the info about Daniel from there, from where he also found out about me and Elisa. He threatens Natalia to get my information, and kills her too.

These were our assumptions, just assumptions, but they made sense than the report on their death certificates.

As we further discussed, the question came: why? And it didn't take that long to find the answer.

"Amy, we have something for you to check," Freya said, handing her the necklace, *the necklace* which could probably be that freak's.

"We found something inside its pendant, a photo, a photo of a woman," Elle completed. The necklace could be of anyone, anyone who lived nearby, but with the slightest chance of it being the hunter's, a possible serial killer having a necklace with a woman's photo, then who might it be?

"Sure enough, now I know why you all looked at me with relief, *relief* which I know was not because we got here safely, give me that."

I watched Amy as she took the necklace and started to search for that woman. Usually, it would've taken her a while to check something like this, but soon after she started, we got the results, a news report – again.

***

WANTED CRIMINAL RUTHEN'S WIFE MURDERED!

January 11th, 2001: Yesterday, January 10th, 2001, the Police got information that the wanted criminal, Ruthen, was found near his own house, and that he might be hiding there. About 5 or 6 in the evening, they let out a sudden mission to arrest Ruthen. There were four officers in charge of the mission: Austin Alexander, William Dormen, Samuel Smith, and Benjamin West. During the mission, William Dormen accidentally shot at Ruthen's wife, Julia, who was pregnant. Police dropped the mission immediately and took Julia to Good Life hospital, but unfortunately, both Julia and the baby died. The criminal Ruthen had gotten away. The officers in charge are temporarily suspended. Higher officials have promised they would carefully consider the situation and would take further appropriate steps.

***

No, this can't be, the officers, Oh my –

I looked at everyone else in terror. Not just in the terror that our parents had killed someone, accidentally, terror that I have seen the man on the screen, right under the report, the criminal, Ruthen, something was inside my head right now, something, a voice? No, Yes, my father's, we were playing the word jumbling game, I was good at it… especially good.

R-U-T-H-E-N

H-U-N-T-E-R

The same letters, but no, in a different order, and Oh that face, it was the video, the video of the fire, one of those who passed the camera while rushing out, that was him, that was my first time seeing him, right? No, not right, somewhere else… yes, that ice cream shop, I've seen him there, right? Amy was going to the counter where he was standing, to get her second ice cream, yeah, right before… that lady came, *that lady with my mother's voice came.*

Everyone else worked it out as soon as I did. Elle was frightened. "Em, My– My father, He shot." Tears were running down her cheeks. I hugged her. My phone tripped from my hands. An incoming call, from an unknown caller, and I was sure who it was, so I picked up the call.

"We found the King, you idiot, now, have you got enough? Enough seeing us rot?!" I yelled.

"Em… It's me," A voice, soft enough, the voice was concerned, a familiar voice, a familiar pause, a familiar addressing, or was it all my imagination?

"Ma?" I replied, Oh hell no, it can't be, it can't be right?

"Yes, yes, I'm here, sweetie, I'm here, are you?" No, this wasn't it, Amy grabbed the phone from me.

"Who are you? Now, whoever this is, you have to know that we can report you for prank calling and causing emotional damage, the technology's good enough nowadays that we can track you right.

"Oh, Amy, Darling, I know it's hard to digest, it's hard for me to explain too, I can't explain it right now, now, you remember the gift I got you right?" That was all, and she hung up.

"Hello? Hello?" But no one answered. I looked at Lena, the gift, the talking teddy.

CHAPTER 31

March 24, 4:32 am

We are now driving to our old house, we never sold it, Aunt never did. We've never returned, not to the house; it was something we left behind, like we never lived there, like we were not born here. Aunt made us forget everything that happened here, well, everything except that our parents died here.

The car was oddly silent, it's like a Déjà vu, or maybe they call it history repeating? Maybe. Because this was the same way we left here, silent, through the exact same paths. Though the city has changed a lot, I guess these paths haven't.

***

The car pulled over in front of our house. I expected it to be a little haunted, but it didn't. It was lively, not like someone hadn't lived here for years. We entered the house, but this time, it was *really* strange, strangely clean, like someone had been living here. I tried to erase the sound of the lady, *who sounded like my mom*, from my mind, but it just doesn't go away.

We walked in and out of the rooms, where once we lived, cried, laughed, and played. The house was still the same, the same. We didn't take anything when we left, except for clothes. Walking in and out of rooms, still looking for that teddy, the one that talks, the one we fought for.

My phone screen lit up with a new message, not from the number that had been messaging us, another one.

*'Find it Quick! Or who knows, maybe it will –
Boom!'*

Our faces changed really quickly. Was it a trap? But even then, we have to find it – I have to find it. This is not just about a freak who letters us, it's about our parents, the pieces were clear now. He is taking revenge for his wife and his baby.

He killed three people; he wouldn't be scared to kill six more. The time was short, though we were not sure how much we had. We began to search the house, this time, frantically.

It was me, I found the teddy. "Hey! Here, I found it! Come here," I yelled. A voice recorder played in the background; it was recorded in the talking teddy. It was my mother's voice, this time, I was sure of it.

Em, if you're hearing this, then you might have regained your memory, or…I may have died. But now, I think it's time for you to know this, we... never had the accident, nor did we die. We faked it… for us, for you all. About 21 years ago, your father, uncle Ben, uncle Sam, and uncle Will went to catch a criminal, but…he didn't mean it, of course, he didn't, uncle Will, he shot at the criminal's wife, who was pregnant, though they took her to the hospital right away, both she and her baby died.

It was a tragic accident…an accident, but it took many lives, not just that woman and her baby's, that criminal, he began hunting our family, and the first victims were, William's brother and his wife, but there was another person in the car when he planned the accident, Will's nephew, Daniel, but he survived, we saved him, and made the media believe he was dead, so that, that criminal would leave him away, we hid him in an orphanage, he was only 2, so we didn't tell him anything, we couldn't keep him either, or he might have known.

That was when we realized he won't let our family off the hook, so your father and others quit their job at the station, so did we quit our jobs on our town and then flew to this city, so that we could hide from him, and we did, for years, we had you, and our lovely other three, Elisa, Amy and Lena. That was when we wanted you to live…not like us, hiding the whole life, we wanted you all to be safe from him, and we knew a few days ago that he had spotted us, again.

We can't take the risk and hide again, then he will know of your existence. We can't let him know about you all, or he will kill you, too. So, some days ago, we faked an

So, my mother… she, she had been alive all this time? She… is she, is she the one who messaged us? The whole message, the one that led us to Alice, the one that warned Daniel, so…all this time?

Daniel froze. I mean, all this time, his parents had died in an accident, but now, they were the poor victims, victims of someone else's actions.

But there was no time for this, no time to grieve. We heard a blasting sound, and a flash, no, it wasn't our house, even worse, did that come from the school's direction? Oh no, it couldn't be… it couldn't be. We ran outside. The school was on fire, people were screaming, we rushed towards the school, people were rushing in, trying to save people, we did too, but it was useless, the place was fully blown up, they were all children… children of five or six age. Blood and grief filled the room instead of smoke. They also had dreams, didn't they? They might have also answered the question "Who do you want to be when you grow up?" They might have had different answers for it, right? They might have been thinking about returning to home, *home*. That merciless creature.

"Come out, you coward!" I yelled, standing in the middle of a burned building, in a room filled with smoke – no grief, Elle and Daniel were with me, others were out saving children. "No one would have died; they would have grown up, like they were supposed to."

"But my child didn't!" A voice came from behind, it was him, Ruthen. "My baby didn't even get to see the world!" He yelled.

"You left none, did you…" I whispered, my eyes glancing through the room, the poor children, "Now tell me the tears you have ever shed aren't just salt water, which is also probably running through your veins instead of blood!"

"And you, you don't deserve that name, that was supposed to be my daughter's name, we, Julia and I, had planned to name her Emma, but, but those brats, they didn't even let us have a chance to look at her for at least once! They were clever. When they knew I wouldn't leave any of them, they ran, escaped. But it was bold for them to hide their kids. It took me this many years to find out about your existence. Alice was just one of my pawns; it didn't take me that much to manipulate her. Now that doesn't matter anymore… because you all aren't going to leave this place."

My body became numb, now I know who I'm named after, the one that left a mark on my parents' hearts, no, not a mark.

A scar.

Someone didn't let him finish, a hit on his head, that was my father, along with my mother, uncle Will, uncle Ben, and Aunt Elsa.

"Run!' My mother yelled, but I was too stunned, too stunned to see my father and mother again. I wanted to hug them, hug them tight once more, but Daniel stopped me.

"We have to save first, Emma!" He grabbed my hand and ran out of the room, and so did others. I tried to go back, I truly couldn't leave them there, with Ruthen. No matter what they have done in the past, they are still the same in my mind. My father wasn't a policeman who ran errands, fighting the culprits. He was just my Dad, who would accompany me through my days and fill them with puzzles and games. My Mom was just my mother, sweet and caring, who would carry my school bag when I came home from school. Sudden screams came from the room not long after we left. I looked back, then ran towards the room.

We ran inside the room, but there was another pool of blood, Ruthen was lying on the floor, *dead*. My dad and others were severely. Uncle Ben was unconscious. Aunt Elsa had a stab. Uncle Will was lying on the floor. Elle rushed towards him, Amy towards Uncle Ben, and Lena towards her mother. They hugged each other in tears. I hugged my mother and father, quickly picking up my phone to call an ambulance, but my dad stopped me.

"Em, don't bother, we won't make for sure," he said, taking my hand.

"No! What are you talking about? Don't talk nonsense now. I just got you all back, but now… No, you're not, we will live together again, as a family, with Aunt Emily–"

"Emily died Em…" My mother cut me off. "So did Sarah, and Samuel, they –" Mom couldn't talk anymore; she spat blood.

"They, they died in our attempt to run away, some accidents, some unexpected diseases, they took them, they're no more, and we… aren't going to make it either." Dad finished mom's sentence.

No, I wasn't going to give them up. Daniel had called the ambulance, and some nurses came and took them away. Elle and I clung to our parents. Daniel pulled me from behind, hugged me as I burst out of tears. Behind me were Elle and others, crying too.

CHAPTER 32

March 25, 7:56 am

This feeling was familiar, for now has repeated 10 years ago, just like Déjà vu. In the graveyard, in front of two graves, Austin Alexander and Amanda Elizabeth. Lying on flowers, I stood, but that day, there was no one beside me. This time, Daniel stood beside me. The feeling of loss wasn't new to him either, was it?

"The fate is so fierce for us, isn't it? You just got your parents back, and now –" He said in a low voice.

"No it isn't, in some way, I want to believe it isn't, they might be free now, in a manner, they don't have to hide now, don't have to try their best to protect their kids from a criminal now, they are free" I said, but those words tasted bitter, I wanted them back, wanted them to come back and hug me once more.

Maybe he knew, he held my hands. "I know you want them back, but they're already here, with you."

I took off my necklace and placed it on top of their graves.

"No pain or regrets will ever feel the same," I turned to him, holding his hand even tighter. "You're right, sometimes, we don't need physical belongings to remember our beloved, they already live in our mind."

ACKNOWLEDGEMENT

Two years ago, I was simply a seventh grader scribbling away on random notes with my friends, crafting a story just to pass the time. Today, I sit here as a ninth grader with a completed novel in front of me. What began as a whim has grown into something I never imagined—and that transformation wasn't mine alone.

First and foremost, I want to thank my parents. Without their constant support, patience, and faith in me, this novel would've stayed buried in my notebook. Writing a book is a whirlwind of emotions, excitement, doubt, and hope, and navigating that as a teenager is no small feat. They didn't dismiss my dream as a passing phase but helped nurture it into reality.

To my dear friends Aksa, Achsah, and Abiya, this story started with you. You weren't just characters in the tale, but pillars in the process. Aksa's encouragement pushed me forward when I doubted myself, and Achsah and Abiya stood by me with unwavering support. To Thanmaya, your small but meaningful gestures kept my hopes alive. Even the idea that someone would read and appreciate this story made all the difference.

A huge thank you to my teachers, who contributed to this journey in ways they may never realize. Linza, the teacher, whose love for books mirrored mine, and who was among the first to hear this story. Arunima's sister, who assured us things would work out even when publishing felt overwhelming and impossible. My Biny teacher, who sparked my fascination for English and shaped how I express myself. Rintu teacher, thank you for Ethal—a name you suggested so long ago that still holds a cherished place in my story. Even though I changed the names of characters when I rewrote it, I never changed 'Ethal'.

Special thanks to Ali Marie, author of the books 'A Girl Named Ivy' and 'What Went Wrong Last Summer' and YouTuber, whose videos introduced me to the concept of self-publishing. Her voice of experience and authenticity helped me find a path where I once saw only hurdles.

And finally, thank you—to you, the reader. If you've made it this far into the book, whether you adored it or just gave it a chance, I am endlessly grateful. Knowing that even one person enjoyed my story brings me more joy than I can express. Your time, attention, and imagination are gifts I treasure. I'm grateful that you gave my book a chance, and I'm eager to build on that experience if I get an opportunity to write again.

Christina Binu is a teen author making her debut in the literary world with her first book, 'Solve for X'. Born and raised in Kerala, India, Christina developed a passion for writing at a young age. When not writing, she enjoys doing pencil drawings and digital art.